Sophie's MIXED-UP Magic

Under a Spell

Amanda Ashby

BOOK 2

PUFFIN BOOKS
An Imprint of Penguin Group (USA) Inc.

PUFFIN BOOKS

Published by the Penguin Group

Penguin Young Readers Group, 345 Hudson Street, New York, New York 10014, U.S.A.

Penguin Group (Canada), 90 Eglinton Avenue East, Suite 700,
Toronto, Ontario, Canada M4P 2Y3 (a division of Pearson Penguin Canada Inc.)

Penguin Books Ltd, 80 Strand, London WC2R 0RL, England

Penguin Ireland, 25 St Stephen's Green, Dublin 2, Ireland (a division of Penguin Books Ltd)

Penguin Group (Australia), 250 Camberwell Road, Camberwell, Victoria 3124, Australia
(a division of Pearson Australia Group Pty Ltd)

Penguin Books India Pvt Ltd, 11 Community Centre, Panchsheel Park,
New Delhi - 110 017, India

Penguin Group (NZ), 67 Apollo Drive, Rosedale, Auckland 0632, New Zealand
(a division of Pearson New Zealand Ltd)

Penguin Books (South Africa) (Pty) Ltd, 24 Sturdee Avenue,
Rosebank, Johannesburg 2196, South Africa

Penguin Books Ltd, Registered Offices: 80 Strand, London WC2R 0RL, England

Published by Puffin Books, a member of Penguin Young Readers Group, 2012

1 3 5 7 9 10 8 6 4 2

LIBRARY OF CONGRESS CATALOGING-IN-PUBLICATION DATA IS AVAILABLE.

Puffin Books ISBN 978-0-14-241680-8

Book design by Jeanine Henderson
Text set in Janson

Printed in the United States of America

Acknowledgments

The usual suspects must be listed here because without them this book would just be a big hot mess in my head! To my agent, Jenny Bent, who does everything with style, grace, and candy. To Christina Phillips and Sara Hantz, who read everything I write and probably a lot of things that I shouldn't write. As ever, a big thank-you to Karen Chaplin, who helped bring Sophie to life, and to Kristin Gilson, who took over so seamlessly. Once again to Jeanine Henderson and everyone else who helped create such beautiful covers!

I would also like to thank Michelle Rowen, who didn't even laugh when I sent her a panicked "er, how do you write a series" e-mail. Her advice was priceless and so is she. And finally, to my husband and kids, who are forced to help me brainstorm my books all the time. I'm not saying that I withhold food from them until they get it right; however, I will say that living with a writer can be perilous and they all handle it amazingly well!

T HERE WERE MANY THINGS THAT SOPHIE CAMPBELL was good at; unfortunately, basketball wasn't one of them. In fact, as far as she was concerned, instead of making basketball part of PE, it should be banned on the grounds that it was humiliating and cruel to short people like herself. She had also apparently been at the back of the line when hand-eye coordination was being passed out, which made it even worse. It wasn't like she wasn't a positive person, because she was. A really, really positive person. But seriously, how could anyone be positive when she was surrounded by other people's armpits?

Sophie's two best friends, Kara and Harvey, looked equally unimpressed as they all sat in the bleachers of Robert Robertson Middle School's gym on Monday afternoon, waiting for the ritual humiliation to begin. It was worst for Harvey, who was tall and skinny and looked like he should be able to play. Unfortunately, he tended to think of the ball as a weapon of mass destruction that should be avoided at all costs, which didn't exactly lend itself to success in the sport.

At that moment their PE teacher, Miss Carson, realized that the three of them were still sitting, and she waved for them to come down onto the court.

"And I mean now, Harvey Trenton," the teacher added when Harvey shot her a blank look. He reluctantly untangled his lanky legs, blew his bangs out of his eyes, and jogged over. Sophie and Kara trailed unenthusiastically behind him and joined the rest of the class doing warm-up lunges. Still, not even the prospect of playing basketball could ruin Sophie's mood. Especially when so many great things had happened to her since she had entered sixth grade just over three weeks ago.

For a start, she and her friends were all in the same homeroom (score). Then there was the fact that over the weekend they had managed to get backstage at the Neanderthal Joe concert, where Eddie Henry (the best bass player In. The. World) had given Sophie his guitar pick. And finally, the icing on top of Sophie's deliciously gorgeous pink cupcake was that she and Jonathan Tait had shared "a moment."

It had been just after Eddie had given her the guitar pick. In her excitement Sophie had spilled the contents of her purse, and Jonathan had immediately dropped to the ground to help her gather everything up. *And that's when it happened.* They had both reached for her camera at the same time, causing their fingers to touch. Sophie immediately felt a jolt of electricity go zooming through her, and, as their eyes locked, she tightened her grasp on Jonathan's fingers. It was perfect (and she didn't care what Harvey said, because she knew a moment when she had one, and this most definitely was one).

She let out a dreamy sigh as her fingers tightened around the guitar pick, which was now hanging from her neck on a delicate silver chain. Like she said, a lot had happened in the last few weeks, and—

"Soph, watch out," Kara's voice suddenly cut into her thoughts. Sophie looked up just in time to see a basketball heading straight for her nose.

She instinctively went to lift her hands to stop it from hitting her, but her fingers were tangled in the chain around her neck. There was no way she wanted to break it, but she didn't want to break her face either, which meant there was only one other thing she could do.

She closed her eyes and wished for the ball not to hit her.

A nanosecond later a telltale tingle went racing through her body like a sugar rush, and she saw the ball come to a halt, just inches from her face. It hovered there for what seemed like ten hours before it dropped harmlessly down at her feet.

Oh, she should probably also mention the other thing that had happened since she'd started sixth grade: she had kind of become a djinn.

That's right, a djinn. As in a genie, complete with

magic, orange skin, and immortality. She even had her own ghostly djinn guide called Malik, who was supposed to be showing her the ropes but instead spent most of his time eating Cheetos, downloading stuff from the Internet, and annoying Sophie on a regular basis. And for some weird reason, despite the fact he could shape-shift into anyone he wanted, he had taken to looking like Zac Efron, right down to the streaky caramel-colored hair and navy blue eyes.

At first Sophie had been tempted to take a special reversal pill so that her life could go back to normal. But then she discovered that her dad, who had walked out four years ago, was actually a djinn, too. And so she had kept her powers so that she would be allowed to see the Djinn Council and ask for its help in finding him. Plus, she had to admit that once she'd managed to make her skin look a normal color, being a djinn definitely had its uses. Like stopping flying basketballs and helping her get backstage passes to meet Neanderthal Joe.

"Whoa," one of the jocks said from somewhere behind her. "Like, dude, did that ball just float in the air?"

"What? No," Kara said quickly, since it was important no one found out the truth. Instead, she grabbed the ball and threw it to Harvey (who promptly dropped it). "It most definitely didn't."

"Are you sure? Because it looked like it was floating to me," the jock continued in a loud and very persistent voice.

"Of course she's sure. It was merely gravity. You know, Newton and his whole: 'What goes up must come down' thing," Harvey added as he kicked away the offending basketball. It looked like the jock was going to protest further, but before he could, there was a piercing whistle, and Sophie turned to see Miss Carson glaring at her.

"Sophie Campbell, since you seem to be off in dreamland, I think I'll make you captain of the red team, and you better hope you don't lose or else it will be four laps for you. Understand?" Then, without another word, she threw another basketball directly at Sophie.

At least it wasn't aimed at her face this time, but Sophie wasn't taking any chances. She once again closed her eyes and wished for the ball to slow down before it reached her. However, this time, instead of letting it hover in front of her, she plucked it from the air as if she'd caught it. For a moment Miss Carson almost looked disappointed before she jogged off and began to yell at someone else. Sophie grinned. Perhaps basketball wasn't so bad after all?

"Are you crazy? I thought you weren't going to do any magic where people could see you," Harvey demanded in a low voice as they shuffled around the court, making sure that they avoided the ball and some of their more zealous classmates. "Because, news flash, lots of people just saw your little display."

"I didn't plan to," Sophie protested. "But then Miss Carson tried to throw a ball in my face. What was that about?"

"I think she's gone Dark Side." Kara pushed a stray strand of long hair back off her face and shuddered. "As in, she's now dating Señor Rena."

"That explains a lot." Sophie nodded as she ducked out of the way of another flying ball. Despite being at school for only three weeks, she had already managed to annoy her Spanish teacher in a major way, and now he was obviously going for some payback by bad-mouthing her to everyone else.

"But Harvey's right," Kara, who never liked to hurt anyone, reluctantly agreed. "I thought the idea was to be more careful with your magic. What if someone had figured it out?"

"Then I'm sure Malik would've taught me some magic to fix that as well," Sophie said in a positive voice. "Besides, what's the point of having loads of awesome powers if I can't use them to fix things? Or, in this case, to stop myself from getting a broken nose?"

"Okay fine. But just be more careful next time," Harvey said as the bell finally rang and they were allowed to jog off court to the safety of the bleachers. "Anyway, are we still okay to go to the library and work on this history assignment? Because I swear that this time I really am going to fail. I don't even know the difference between World War I and World War II."

"About twenty years for a start," Sophie told him before giving him a reassuring smile. "And yes, the library is definitely still on." Especially since, despite history being her favorite subject, she hadn't started her own assignment either. Unfortunately, for some unknown reason, the only thing she couldn't really use her magic on was homework. Well, she kind of could, but only if she had done the research first, which seemed a bit pointless.

"Thanks, Sophie," Harvey said. But before she could answer him, Kara's cell phone beeped, and her friend quickly pulled it from her pocket and studied the screen. Sophie was immediately distracted as her heart pounded with nerves and excitement.

"Any news?" she asked while trying to resist the urge to cross her fingers. Ever since she had discovered the truth about her dad, she had been trying to get an appointment with the Djinn Council so that the members could open up a special djinn safe-deposit box that he had left her. However, despite Malik going to see them last week, Sophie was still waiting to hear back. It was definitely starting to grate on her.

Even worse, she was the only sixth grader without a cell phone, and all her plans to conjure one up had been nixed by Malik on the grounds that her mom wouldn't like it. She had tried to point out that her mom probably wouldn't like Sophie being a djinn either, but Malik wouldn't listen, and he had totally guilt-tripped her out of doing it. Of course it hadn't stopped him from getting one for himself, and he had promised to send Kara a text message if he had heard anything.

"No. I'm sorry. It's just about a stagehand meeting

tomorrow. It's going to be in the art room instead of the auditorium," Kara explained. Kara was an art buff and had recently signed up to help make the backgrounds and props for the upcoming musical, *The Wizard of Oz*.

"Oh." Sophie tried to bite back her disappointment while reminding herself that she was a positive person. However, before she could say anything else, there was a rustling of wings, and a gigantic pink pigeon suddenly appeared in the middle of the basketball court.

Sophie had seen pink pigeons before, when she'd ordered things from Rufus's Bazaar, but Kara and Harvey hadn't, which would explain why they were frozen to the spot. Thankfully, the gym was otherwise empty, and Sophie hurried toward the bird, trying to figure out if she'd ordered anything djinn-related recently. However, on account of spending the last of her pocket money at the Neanderthal Joe concert, she was pretty sure that she hadn't.

As she got closer, she could see that the bird was holding a letter in its beak (and glaring at her, all at the same time). She tentatively held out her hand to get the letter, but before she could, the bird took a step away and made a snorting noise. She turned to Harvey.

"Do you have any snacks in your bag? It won't complete the delivery unless it's given a tip, but unfortunately, it refuses to eat conjured-up food. Malik says it's just being contrary, but I don't want to risk offending it."

"Oh." Harvey didn't look happy as he reluctantly undid his backpack. "Well, I guess I have a Mars bar, but I was saving it up for the library. Are you sure you need it? I mean, for all we know the bird is just delivering some junk mail?"

"Harvey," Kara interjected before Sophie could say anything. "Just give her the candy."

"Fine," Harvey grumbled as he passed it over and narrowed his eyes at the pink pigeon. The bird ignored him as Sophie gingerly held out the candy bar and crossed her fingers that it wouldn't bite her. (It would be bad enough to be bitten by a regular overweight pigeon. Being bitten by a pink one would be just a bit too much.)

Thankfully, the bird seemed happy with the exchange. A second after swiping the candy bar from her hand, it disappeared from sight, leaving them alone with the letter.

"Wow." Kara let out a small gasp. "That was crazy. So was Harvey right? Is it just some djinn junk mail?"

Sophie hardly heard as her fumbling fingers finally smoothed down the piece of paper and studied the name that ran along the top in a lavish cursive that Sophie could barely read. She took a deep breath and turned back to her friends.

"It's from the Djinn Council."

Kara and Harvey were immediately at Sophie's side as they peered over her shoulder so that they could read it:

Dear Initiate,

Your request to meet with the Djinn Council has been approved. However, since you failed to file a P78U before you made the application, you will have to undergo a Phoe‑nician test to prove that you are magically adept in order for the interview to take place. You will present yourself to us on the third moon of the Agate quarter. You are also required to bring sensible shoes and a raincoat, and upon entering the council chambers, you will sign a 9GJH7 to state that you accept full responsibility for anything that might happen to you during the course of your interview.

Yours,

Leshanka the Odious

Djinn Council General Undersecretary and Translator

For a moment Sophie just stared at the letter as her heart started to pound. They were going to see the Djinn Council, which meant that *she was going to find her dad*. She was going to find her dad! She read the letter again as Kara coughed in her ear.

"What's a Phoenician test?" Her friend wrinkled her nose.

"And when's the third moon of the Agate quarter when we're at home?" Harvey added.

"I've got no idea," Sophie admitted, visions of her dad still consuming her mind. "But I know someone who will. Malik."

She clapped her hands as a tremor of excitement mixed

with panic went racing through her. Thanks to being such a positive thinker, she had always known that her dad must have had a very good reason for leaving them (of course, at the time she had thought it was most likely because he had amnesia or temporary insanity rather than because he was a djinn). But that was beside the point. All that mattered now was that soon she would find out what had happened. *And find out where he was.*

No wonder she felt funny, since this could end up being the most memorable day of her life. However, after five more minutes of clapping and rereading the letter from the Djinn Council, there was still no sign of Malik. She looked up at her friends.

"Are you guys okay if I bail on the library? I'm going to go crazy if I can't find out what this letter means. If Malik's not at home, I can e-mail Rufus and ask him."

"Of course. You should go already," Kara instantly assured her. Harvey looked a bit worried since he really hadn't been joking about his needing help at history, but he nodded his head anyway.

"Thanks." Sophie shot them each a grateful look and quickly zapped Harvey a replacement Mars bar (plus one for Kara). Then, without another word, she raced to the locker room to get changed. The sooner she got home, the sooner she could find her dad.

I'M GOING TO FIND HIM. I'M GOING TO FIND HIM," Sophie chanted to herself as she hurried off the bus and raced toward her house. "I mean, how can I not find him when I'm such a positive person? *A strong, lucky, positive person who is going to find out what happened to her dad, and—*"

"Did you say something?" A seventh grader with sandy blond hair and shoulders the size of a mountain suddenly turned around and looked at her with interest. Sophie groaned as she realized it was Ben Griggs, who was not only a friend of Jonathan Tait's but, if rumors were to be believed, was also Melissa Tait's boyfriend. At this point she should probably mention that, due to a minor misunderstanding involving a pair of designer jeans, Jonathan's (evil) twin sister, Melissa, hated Sophie with a passion. Which, in other words, meant that Ben Griggs was the perfect person to catch her talking to herself. Not.

She felt her face heat up in embarrassment.

"Oh, er, I was just practicing for an English assignment," she quickly explained while she made a mental note to stop chanting positive affirmations when she was out in public. It would probably help if she could stop blushing so much as well.

"Rrrrright." Ben started to roll his green eyes as if she was the biggest moron he had ever seen. Suddenly he caught sight of the guitar pick that was hanging around her neck. "Oh, hey, I know you—you're the girl who got JT and his brother backstage at the Neanderthal Joe gig on Saturday."

"That's right," Sophie agreed, since she was hardly going to mention that the thing that actually let Jonathan and his older brother go backstage with them was the djinn magic she used to put the mojo on their tickets. Because really, details, schmetails. The important thing was that Jonathan had obviously told his friends about her. She immediately brightened.

"Sweet." Ben nodded. "So, is it true that Eddie Henry really gave you that guitar pick?"

Sophie nodded and held the necklace up so he could see it more clearly, just like she'd been doing all day to the procession of kids who had wanted to catch a glimpse of it. Harvey had even joked that she should start charging for the privilege.

"Nice." Ben leaned forward and tentatively touched it before he let out a long whistle. However, before he could say anything else, his cell phone beeped. She watched as he pulled it out of his back pocket and studied the screen.

"I gotta blaze, but thanks for letting me touch it. Maybe it will bring me good luck when my mom finds out I flunked my geography test."

Then without another word he jogged off down the street. Sophie blinked. Okay, as far as embarrassing incidents went, that hadn't ended up too badly. And while she wasn't quite sure what boys talked about when they were together, hopefully Ben would tell Jonathan that he had seen her and that she was perfect girlfriend material. The idea made Sophie grin as she hurried the rest of the way to her house.

Once she got there, she paused for a moment at the end of the path, pleased that it *was* still her house. Her mom, while suffering from a major freak-out, had almost sold it so that they could all move to Montana (exactly). Thankfully, she had changed her mind at the last minute. Now, every time Sophie saw the house she let out a little prayer of gratitude that they still lived there.

It had once been a nice two-story white weatherboard house, but ever since her dad left it had been showing signs of neglect: peeling paint, overgrown garden beds, and...*a recently deceased djinn called Malik standing on the front porch peering in through the window?*

Okay, so the last part definitely wasn't a regular fixture.

"Malik," Sophie called out in a low voice. "Malik," she tried again, but when there was still no answer, she clapped her hands together. He immediately disappeared from his spot by the window and reappeared next to her on the path. Sophie couldn't help but wish that he always came that quickly when she summoned him.

"Oh, hey, Sophie, there you are," he said in a cheery voice, as if it was completely normal for him to be standing on her porch, staring in through her front window (which, for the record, it was not). What was normal was that he still looked like Zac Efron's döppelganger.

"What are you doing?" she demanded in a low voice. "I've been clapping you over and over again. Why didn't you come?"

"Oh, yes, sorry about that." He shot her an apologetic look as he nodded up to the house. "It's just…it's your mom. I'm a bit worried about her."

"My mom? What's wrong with her?" Sophie's mouth immediately went dry, and all thoughts of the Djinn Council letter faded from her mind and were replaced by one of panic. "D-did something happen when I was at school? Did you say something weird to her on Facebook?"

"What? Of course not," Malik replied, sounding offended. "Why would I say something weird to her? Besides, I haven't seen her online in days. In fact, at first I thought that the problem was that she was missing my charismatic, charming personality."

"She thinks you're a divorcée called MG who wears dresses and likes cooking," Sophie reminded him as she tried not to think of the fact that Malik had a crush on her mom and flirted with her on Facebook any chance he could get. It was just so gross on way too many levels.

"Oh, I think that subconsciously she knows the truth," Malik assured her as he puffed out his chest. "Anyway I don't like to alarm you, but I think she's dying."

"What?" Sophie felt like she had been hit in the stomach. Hard.

For a moment she wondered if she was going to faint, and she desperately willed herself to stay calm, but it was hard. After all, for four years she'd been waiting for her dad to come home so that they could be a real family again. She'd never thought she had to worry about her—

"Your mom," Malik repeated in a loud, clear voice, as if she hadn't heard him correctly the first time. "We're talking about your mom and how I think she's dying. I mean, she keeps pacing up and down the room, and there has been a lot of arm flailing and wailing. Humans are so frail and mortal. Do you think it's some kind of flesh-eating disease?" Malik wondered aloud. Sophie ignored him as she hurried up the wide porch steps and over to the large glass window.

Her heart was pounding as she peered inside, and she tried not to panic. Her mom was wearing an old blue shirt that had once belonged to Sophie's dad. But for whatever reason, instead of working, she was marching back and forth across the already well-worn Turkish rug. Sophie anxiously studied her mom's face for any sign of illness.

"See." Malik was suddenly next to her. "I mean, there's

definitely something wrong with her. Of course I might be mistaken about the flesh-eating disease, but I think you'd better get her to the hospital quickly. Maybe it's a heart attack? Or acute kidney failure?"

"Actually." Sophie pressed her nose up to the glass and studied her mom. People often said they looked alike, with the same straight blonde hair and freckles, though right now something was different. Sophie squinted. "She doesn't look sick, she looks… *annoyed*?"

"Annoyed?" Malik looked at her with interest. "Why? I wonder what you've done now?"

"What do you mean? I haven't done anything," Sophie protested as she continued to study her mom's face. Yup, she was definitely annoyed.

"Are you sure?" Malik double-checked. "Because you know how she worries about you… oh, hang on a moment, she's seen you, and now she's coming over. How do I look?"

"Like an invisible ghost with bad taste in shirts," Sophie retorted in a dry voice just as her mom looked out the window and caught sight of her. She immediately marched over and threw open the window.

"Sophie Charlotte-Marie Campbell! I've been waiting for you to come home from school. In here now, please," her mom said in a tight voice as she did that thing with her lips that could mean only one thing. Trouble.

"I-is something wrong?" Sophie gulped while Malik carefully smoothed his bright purple Hawaiian shirt and then gave her mom a coy little half wave. Sophie glared at him as she opened the front door and went into the dining room. Her mom was waiting for her.

When her dad had still been at home, the dining room was used a lot, but these days the long mahogany table mainly served to house bills, old magazines, and, on occasion, the large cardboard sharks that her younger sister, Meg, liked to make. It was also where Sophie had escaped to last night in an attempt to start her history assignment.

However, right now the place was a total mess.

The normal junk from the table was strewn across the floor, and in its place was a collection of empty, up-ended CD and DVD cases. The discs themselves were scattered everywhere like fallen stars, twinkling and gleaming in the late-afternoon sunshine, which was pushing its way in through a large window.

"Boy, now that's what I call a mess." Malik let out a long whistle that no one but Sophie could hear. She ignored him as she turned back to her mom.

"What happened here?" Sophie blinked, still trying to take it all in.

"I was hoping that you would tell me." Her mom folded her arms.

"I don't have a clue." Sophie shook her head, since while she had been in there last night all she had done was re-live the Neanderthal Joe concert in her mind (hence, her history assignment still wasn't started). "But I can promise it wasn't me. Why don't you ask Meg? You know what she and Jessica are like once they start playing together."

"Oh, will you look at that?" Malik finally glanced at an imaginary watch on his wrist. "Is that the time? Because you know what? I really need to fly—well, not fly, since I'm a ghost not a bird—but still, I really need to get gone from here. Talksoonbye," he finished off in a rush. Before Sophie could even think of throwing something at him, he disappeared from sight. She reluctantly turned back to where her mom was impatiently staring at her.

"Well?" Her mom repeated as she tapped her foot on the carpet. "Are you going to tell me what happened?"

There was nothing Sophie would have liked more, but unfortunately, that wasn't exactly an option. At that moment her six-year-old sister, Meg, suddenly appeared from the kitchen with a PB&J sandwich in her hand. Despite her blonde ringlets and large kewpie-doll eyes, Meg's favorite thing in the world was watching shark attacks. Though judging by the excited gleam in her sister's eyes, watching Sophie get in trouble was a close second.

Hard on Meg's heel was Mr. Jaws, a black-and-white cat who, no matter how much Sophie bribed him with Kitty Crunch, kept hissing at her and Malik every time he saw them. Thankfully, no one paid any attention to him, or else Sophie would've been in big trouble. *Well*, she amended, *bigger trouble than she was in right now.*

"Okay," Sophie forced herself to lie as she realized her mom was still waiting for an answer. "You're right. It was

me. I was looking for my iPod. I-I couldn't find it anywhere. I'm sorry."

"You know," her mom said as her anger seemed to
give way to disappointment. "I really thought that, once I
started doing my pottery again, you girls would help out
more around the house, but instead I get this."

"You're not going to change your mind about selling
the house, are you?" Meg yelped in alarm while simultaneously glaring at Sophie as if it was all her fault.

"No." Her mom shook her head. "But I'm serious about
needing more help. I've got to finish my order, and I still
can't find the new pottery glaze I bought yesterday. You
haven't taken it, have you?"

"Of course not." Sophie blinked. "Why would I want
your pottery glaze?"

"Same reason you felt obliged to make this mess," her
mom retorted. "Anyway, if I'm going to get everything
done, then I'm going to need your help, which means that
you can clean this mess up while I keep looking for my
glaze."

"What?" Sophie protested. It was one thing to confess
to a crime that you didn't commit, but it was another thing
entirely to have to tidy up after it. Then she remembered
that she was a djinn now and all she had to do was wish for
the mess to be gone and it would be. "Okay, fine. I'll tidy
it up," she relented.

"Thank you." Her mom looked tired, and Sophie suddenly felt a flash of guilt run through her. The last four

years, since her dad had gone, things had been tough on them all. One of the reasons her mom had wanted to move was because she had been getting so stressed out.

Still, Sophie would soon know exactly where her dad was, and then everything would be better. And in the meantime, it would take only one second to clean up this mess, and she would still have time to finish her history research so that she could conjure up an assignment and then kill Malik. All before dinner.

She waited until her mom had headed back out to her pottery shed and was just about to wish for the room to be tidied up when she realized that Meg and Mr. Jaws were still in the room staring at her like they'd just bought front-row tickets.

"Er, Meg, don't you have anything better to do than just stand there?" Sophie asked.

"Nope." Meg shook her head and took another bite of her sandwich.

"Let me rephrase that. Can you please go away?"

"Again on the nope." Meg smiled, and Sophie folded her arms in exasperation, since she could hardly work her magic if her kid sister and a bad-tempered cat were watching her.

"But you must have something to do," she wheedled. "What about going next door and playing with Jessica?"

"I hate Jessica Dalton," Meg informed her in a blunt voice as she pulled out one of the heavy dining room chairs and made herself comfortable. "She said that if a dinosaur and a killer shark had a fight that the dinosaur would win. I mean, seriously: a dinosaur beat a killer shark? Not likely. So I told her that she had better take it back or else. But she wouldn't take it back, so now I hate her. Anyway, I'd much rather watch you clean up all this mess."

Sophie let out a long groan as she realized that there was no way she could use her magic now. Instead, she was going to have to do it the old-fashioned way. Great.

S O, I THINK THAT WENT REASONABLY WELL," MALIK said an hour later as Sophie pushed open her bedroom door and collapsed onto her cast-iron bed. Normally, the yellow-and-white wallpapered room soothed her, but right now her back ached, her hands hurt, and she was pretty sure that half of her brain had leaked out of her ears while she had been forced to listen to Meg complain about all the crimes that her former BFF Jessica had committed against her (ranging from scissors stealing to purposely yawning when Meg was having her turn at show-and-tell).

"What?" Sophie struggled back up into a sitting position and glanced over to where Malik was standing, staring at himself in her mirror. "Are you serious? I got the blame for something that *you* did and then had to spend an hour cleaning it up—the hard way, since Meg wouldn't go away and so I couldn't use any magic. How is that good?"

"Well, it's good that your mom isn't dying," he pointed out in a sunny voice as he started to do some kind of pop-

and-lock dance move. It wasn't a success. "Instead, she's just really, really mad at you."

"Oh, yes, I can see how that is so much better," Sophie retorted as she studied the large apple-shaped, rhinestone-studded ring on her finger.

It was actually the ring that was responsible for her djinn powers. When she had first started wearing it (after Malik had tricked her into putting it on), it had been agony to take off, but now that she had learned to control her powers, she could slip it off without aching or screaming. Not that she did very often, since it was amazing just how many adorable outfits a large apple-shaped, rhinestone-studded ring went with.

"I knew you'd understand." Malik beamed.

"Anyway, what happened to the rule of you not going anywhere in the house but my room?" Sophie wanted to know.

"Oh, right." Malik finally turned around, and she realized he was wearing a black hat set at a jaunty angle. "Well, I was doing that, but then I got bored. And hungry. So I thought I'd have a look around, and then I found a movie called *High School Musical* that I was in! Unfortunately, when I went to watch the next one, the disc wasn't in the case, so I had to go through all the DVDs until I found it."

Sophie blinked. "Okay, so I've just spent an hour cleaning up a big mess all because you couldn't find *High School Musical Two*, the movie that your döppelganger Zac Efron stars in?"

"That's correct," Malik agreed before shooting her a reassuring smile. "But don't worry, because in the end I found it stuck behind the DVD player and the crisis was averted. Though you really should talk to your sister about making sure she puts the DVDs away properly. It could've gotten scratched or something."

"I think that was probably the intention," Sophie said, since their grandmother had given Meg all three movies in hopes of moving her away from her gruesome love of sharks. Unfortunately, Meg hadn't been remotely taken with the all-singing, all-dancing teenagers and had stubbornly refused to watch them. Then Sophie noticed that Malik had pinned up a picture of Zac Efron over her favorite Neanderthal Joe poster.

She was pretty sure that in some countries that was a crime punishable by death. She marched across the room and removed the offending poster so that she could once again see the Joes in their full glory. Then she turned back to Malik.

"I'm starting to think it's about time you changed into someone else besides Zac Efron."

"Why would I do that?" Malik wrinkled his Zac nose in confusion. "I mean, Zac is the man. He can sing, he can dance, and his hair is extraordinary. The only problem is that now that I'm no longer a djinn, Zac's a lot oranger than I am. I think it's his fake tan. I don't suppose you could hustle me up some color, could you?"

"What?" Sophie blinked at him, while secretly

wondering how he could still manage to surprise her.

"Color," Malik repeated as he held out his arm and gave a decisive sniff. "I mean, if there's one thing I resent about being dead, it's that I'm no longer orange. I tell you, it's a real blow. Anyway, I've been trying some different paints, but it's just not the same." As he spoke, Sophie realized that there was indeed a collection of paint pots sitting on her bookshelf and that Malik's arm was dotted with various shades of orange, making him look like an anemic tiger.

"I'm not going to turn you orange," Sophie informed him in a blunt voice. "And you have to realize that you can't just wander around the house as you please. My mom's still totally stressed out, and until we find my dad and get him back here, I don't want to make things any worse."

"Of course I wouldn't do anything to make it worse. Your poor mother is totally overwrought. She actually just sent me a message on Facebook to tell me about the dreadful mess you made in the dining room."

"*You* made," Sophie corrected.

"Whatever." Malik gave a dismissive wave of his arm before shooting her a serious look. "The point is that I would never do anything to upset her. Now, about the orange thing. It really is very simple, and it would only take you about an hour to do. Three tops. You do have some ground quartz crystals, don't you?"

"No, I don't, and please stop distracting me. I need to

show you something," Sophie said as she suddenly remembered that in all the drama of thinking her mom was
sick, she still hadn't shown him the letter from the Djinn
Council. She carefully pulled it out of her pocket and
held it out to him. When he finished reading it, he looked
up, his Zac-like eyebrows knitted together and his lips in
a tight line.

"Outrageous," he spluttered as he began to float around
the room, his arms crossed in annoyance. "Those bureau-
cratic old women. I mean, seriously, if you'd seen how big
a P78U is, you would understand why I didn't fill it in. It
was longer than *War and Peace*. And as for making you
take a Phoenician test, that's just plain rude."

"Yes, but what is it?" Sophie asked, not liking the way
he was now chewing his lip. "Is it hard?"

"Of course not...well, it wouldn't have been hard for
me, but then again, I was a djinn of exceptional abilities
and—"

"Malik," Sophie cut him off. "I mean, will it be hard
for me?"

"Oh, right. My apologies. Anyway, it's a rather old-
fashioned test where the Djinn Council sit around like
the overpaid autocrats that they are while fresh young
djinns have to go and impress them with their dazzling
transcendental conjuring skills. Er, so, remind me again
how far we've progressed on your transcendental conjuring."

"My what?" Sophie looked at him blankly as she tried

to imagine herself doing magic in front of a bunch of djinns. Her palms felt clammy.

"Oh." Malik paused for a moment before taking a deep breath and speaking in a bright voice. "Well, let me tell you about transcendental conjuring. It's exactly like what you do now, but instead of just wishing for an object to come out fully formed, you are trying to control something that already exists and make it bend to your will."

"Hey, I could've used that in gym today when I was trying to stop a basketball from hitting me in the face. All I could do was make it stop in the air. Are you saying that I could've done other things with it?"

"Absolutely." Malik nodded. "You could've sent it up toward the ceiling or in the other direction. Or, if you were Zac Efron, you could've made it spin on your finger."

Sophie was about to explain that making a ball spin on your finger wasn't actually magic, but she thought better of it since she didn't want Malik to go off on another tangent. "And the third moon of the Agate quarter? What's that in plain English?"

"Let's see. *Diamond, quartz, silver,*" Malik chanted as he began to count up his fingers before finally nodding. "By my calculations it's the first Tuesday of the year 2058."

"What?" Sophie yelped before putting her hand over her mouth to stop herself from screaming. Finally, she calmed down long enough to speak as she shot him a pleading look. "No. I can't wait that long. I might be immortal, but my mom and sister aren't. Surely this is some kind of mistake."

"Well, it wouldn't be the first time they've made a mistake," Malik agreed before suddenly seeming to notice her panic. "But relax. I have a buddy on the inside. I once helped him do a halstic curse on a sahir who was giving him grief, and let's just say that as far as halstic curses go, I totally rock. I bet a collector's edition of *Charlie St. Cloud* that I can get your appointment changed."

"That would be fantastic." Sophie let out the breath that she didn't know she had been holding. "So, in the meantime, do you think you can show me how to do this transcendental conjuring?"

"Of course I can. After all, I am a djinn guide of exceptional talents." He patted his chest as he glanced around the room before nodding in the direction of her bed. "Oh, I know, why don't you make that deformed creature fly?"

"What?" Sophie blinked before realizing that Malik was looking over to where her favorite childhood toy was sitting. It had once been an overstuffed pink pig, but over the years it had lost an eye, most of its stuffing, and half an ear. However, despite its battered appearance, it had also helped her through a lot of hard times when her dad had first left. She defensively picked it up and gave it a hug. "You want me to make Mr. Pugsy fly?"

"Ah, yes. Isn't that what I just said?" Malik looked confused for a moment. "Anyway, the trick to doing transcendental conjuring is concentration. You need to really focus on what you want to happen and then visualize every last detail, leaving absolutely nothing to chance. *Oh, and I always like to snap my fingers. It just gives the whole demonstration a bit more pizzazz.* So go on then, why don't you try it?"

Sophie had many reasons why she didn't want to try it, not least because it seemed impossible, but since that wouldn't help her find out about her dad, she pushed her concern to the back of her mind and nodded. Then she took a deep breath and settled Mr. Pugsy back down on the bed. As she stared at him, she tried to imagine him lifting off the bed and up toward the ceiling. She regulated her breathing and waited until a familiar tingle went racing through her.

Once she had the image firmly set in her mind, she snapped her fingers and opened her eyes to see Mr. Pugsy lift an inch off the comforter before falling back down.

"Still keen to have your appointment date changed?" Malik raised an eyebrow, but Sophie ignored him as she closed her eyes and tried it again. This time Mr. Pugsy lifted at least four inches before tumbling back down. But as a positive person, Sophie could only assume that this meant she was getting better.

She was just about to try it for a third time when the cordless phone, which was sitting by her bed, rang. She picked it up, pleased for the distraction, since her brain was already hurting.

"Hey, it's me," Kara said from down the other end of

the line. "I was getting worried that I hadn't heard from you. Is everything okay?"

"Sorry, I should've called you, but I had to spend an hour cleaning up the gigantic mess that *Malik* made." Sophie shot the djinn a pointed look. At the mention of his name Malik looked up with interest.

"Is that Kara on the phone? Ask her if she thinks Zac Efron is a good dancer," he said, but Sophie ignored him as she put her hand up to her ear to cut out what he was saying.

"Anyway, it turns out that Phoenician test is something I need to do to impress the Djinn Council with my magic."

"Oh, well, that's a good thing since you rock at magic," Kara said in a supportive voice, but Sophie shook her head as she looked over to where Mr. Pugsy lay on his side, his single eye peering out at her.

"This is different magic. But don't worry. I'm definitely getting the hang of it. I just need to keep practicing," she said. Then she remembered that she'd left Kara and Harvey in the library, and a flash of guilt went racing through her. "Anyway, enough about me. What happened this afternoon? Was Harvey okay?"

"He's pretty stressed about the project, and you know what he's like when he worries," Kara said, and Sophie nodded her head since, when it came to worrying, Harvey was a gold medalist. None of which was helped by the fact that his folks were on the verge of getting divorced and things were tense at home. "And to make it worse, I had to leave him early to go and see how Colin was getting along."

As part of the stage crew for *The Wizard of Oz*, Kara was working on most of the sets, but she'd taken total ownership of Colin, a very large papier-mâché winged monkey statue.

"It's so weird that Harvey can be so good at math and so bad at history," Sophie noted.

"I know, right," Kara agreed from down the other end of the phone. "Anyway, I told him to IM or call us tonight if he gets stuck on anything and we can . . . hey, why did Malik just send me a text message asking me if I thought that Zac Efron was good looking?" Kara asked in a surprised voice as Sophie turned around to see that Malik had his cell phone out and was busy texting.

"Ignore him," she said as she stalked over and plucked the cell phone out of his hand.

"I was using that," Malik protested.

"Yes, well—" Sophie started to say before she caught sight of a large orange Italy-shaped stain on her carpet just by Malik's foot. Then she spotted a tub of orange pottery glaze that someone (she was going to go out on a limb here and say Malik) had kicked under her dresser. Sophie let out a long groan as she realized it was the pottery glaze her mom had been looking for all afternoon. "You took my mom's glaze?" she squeaked at him.

"Yeah, and you know, I had really high hopes for that

one," Malik confided as he held out his stripy arm. "But unfortunately, it didn't look so good once I got it on. I guess it's made for clay, not ghost skin."

"You think?" Sophie lifted an eyebrow at him, but before she could say anything else Kara piped up.

"What's going on?" her friend demanded in concern.

"Malik's what's going on," Sophie retorted as she told Kara exactly what her troublesome djinn guide had been doing.

"He did all of that in just one day?" Kara exclaimed once Sophie had finished. "Is there a spell to make sure he doesn't cause any more trouble at home? Or maybe send him on vacation for a few weeks just until your mom has finished her pottery order?"

The idea was more than a little tempting, especially since a little bit of Malik could go a long, long way. But before she could say anything she caught sight of the safe-deposit box that her dad had given her just before he left home four years ago. Of course it wasn't until last week that she had learned that her dad was a djinn or that the answers to his mysterious disappearance might be within the small silver box.

Sophie tucked the cordless phone under her ear and wistfully ran her fingers across the box's surface so that the delicate engravings rubbed against her skin, as if willing the box to open up. But no matter what she did, it stayed annoyingly shut.

"I can't." Sophie let out a reluctant sigh. "Since there is

no way I can learn how to do this transcendental conjuring on my own. Plus, I need him to try to get my appointment moved forward."

"I guess." Kara let out a frustrated sigh. "It's like a Catch Twenty-two because you need him to be close by but you can't afford for him to cause any more trouble for your mom. Still, I suppose there isn't much you can do except hope he behaves himself while we're at school each day."

"That's it!" Sophie cried. "Kara, you're a genius. I know exactly what I need to do."

"Turn me orange?" Malik asked in a hopeful voice, but Sophie just shook her head.

"No, I told you I'm not going to turn you orange, but there's no way I can leave you at home causing all sorts of problems. My mom's stressed out enough as it is, and I can't let anything happen until I find out more about my dad. I mean, imagine if I got grounded when I was meant to be seeing the Djinn Council? It would be a disaster. Which means there's only one other solution."

"What?" Kara asked in a cautious voice.

"It's simple. Starting tomorrow Malik will be coming with us to school."

"SOPH, ARE YOU SURE YOU'VE THOUGHT THIS through?" Harvey asked the next morning as he and Kara congregated around Sophie's locker before the first bell. Thanks to Meg's feud with Jessica Dalton, her sister was refusing to be driven to school by Mrs. Dalton. This meant their mom had to drop Meg off, and she had decided that Sophie should go with them. However, judging by Harvey's worried expression, she guessed that Kara had filled him in on what had happened yesterday.

"Of course I'm sure," she assured him.

"But if Malik caused so many problems at your house, can you imagine what he could get up to here?" Harvey continued as he pulled a packet of M&M's out of his pocket and started to fiddle with it (a sure sign he was worried since normally he would just eat the candies).

"It had crossed my mind," Sophie admitted. "But really, the main thing is that my mom can get her pottery order finished without getting stressed out or doing anything crazy like grounding me. It's just I'm so close to finding my dad that I can't afford for anything to go wrong at home. And speaking of my dad, look at this." As she spoke, she nodded for them both to peer into her locker.

Once they were next to her, Sophie concentrated on her science book, which was sitting at the bottom. Just as Malik had taught her, she cleared her mind and felt her breath rising and falling. Then she visualized the book floating into the air. Finally, she clicked her fingers.

She didn't open her eyes, but by the excited gasps next to her, she could tell it was working. She pictured the book opening up and the pages flicking from one side to the other. Again her friends gasped, and then Sophie let the book float back to the bottom of the locker before opening her eyes and grinning at them. She still hadn't managed to get Mr. Pugsy to lift up more than a foot from the bed, but when it came to making books fly, she ruled.

"Wow," Kara said in awe, while next to her Harvey was nodding his head in agreement. "You learned how to do that in one night?"

Sophie nodded. "I had to bribe Malik with far too many Cheetos and Zac Efron DVDs, but he eventually managed to talk me through it. Now I just need to keep practicing as much as I can. Apparently, the next step is to move from inanimate objects like books and pens to myself. I'm not really sure I want to float, but Malik has assured me that's the best way to impress the council."

"Floating?" Harvey looked excited. "Can you make *me*

float? Because I'd definitely be interested in that, and... hey, why is Ben Griggs waving at you?"

"What?" Sophie and Kara immediately glanced over to where Ben was most definitely waving at her like they were long-lost BFFs. Unlike Melissa Tait, who was standing next to him looking all sour and ticked off.

"Okay, so that's weird," Kara said in surprise. "Since when do you know Ben Griggs?"

"Yeah, because I don't mean to be a downer, but that guy is a total contender for Moron of the Year," Harvey informed her. "Not to mention that he likes beating up on sixth graders. Oh, and don't get me started on his aggressive body language. I mean, look at the way he's standing, and how his eyebrows are cocked. You really shouldn't hang out with people who have cocked eyebrows, Sophie."

That was the other thing about Harvey. Ever since his folks had started fighting he had become obsessed with body language and trying to figure out what it all meant.

"I don't hang out with him. I don't even know him," Sophie protested before suddenly remembering what happened on the way home yesterday. "Well, I didn't, but when I was walking from the bus, he kind of heard me doing some affirmations. Anyway, we talked for a couple of minutes, but I don't get why he would be waving at me."

"I think you're going to find out really soon." Harvey nodded as Ben Griggs started to jog toward them. "But if he says anything about beating up sixth graders, I think you should turn him into a toad. Okay?"

"Of course he's not going to try to beat any of us up," Sophie assured him before catching his worried look. She let out a reluctant sigh. "Fine. If he even looks at you funny, then he will be totally toadified."

"Toadified? Is that even a word?" Kara asked. But before Sophie could answer, Ben had closed the distance between them and suddenly he was standing there, once again staring directly at her.

"Hey, Campbell," the seventh grader said. "I was hoping to catch you before first period."

"You were?" Sophie blinked in surprise. Next to her Harvey and Kara looked equally confused. "Er, why?"

"To say thank you for letting me touch Eddie Henry's guitar pick yesterday. You know I was hoping it would bring me good luck when I told my mom about flunking my test? Well, it totally did. I mean, she didn't even yell or anything. And this is a woman who likes to yell."

"Oh. Okay. Well, that's good. I mean, no one likes to be yelled at," she said in a polite voice, still not quite sure she followed what he was saying.

"I know, right." Ben gave an eager nod of his head. "Anyway, the thing is that I've got to go see Principal Gerrard. She's kind of annoyed at me for setting fire to my lab partner yesterday."

"You set your lab partner on fire?" Kara suddenly squeaked, while next to her Harvey started to have a coughing fit and Sophie was pretty sure she heard him muttering the words *turn the pyro into a toad* under his breath.

"It was a total accident, and no skin was burned," Ben assured her, not looking remotely remorseful. Then he shot her a pleading smile. "It's just Principal Gerrard doesn't seem to see it that way, so I was kind of hoping I could touch the guitar pick again."

For a moment Sophie paused. It wasn't that she particularly liked Ben Griggs—dating Melissa Tait and setting his lab partner on fire weren't the kind of qualities she admired in a person. However, he was a friend of Jonathan Tait's, and there was no way she wanted to offend him. She found herself nodding her head.

"Sure. I mean, yeah. I guess." She reluctantly pulled out the necklace from under her shirt. The minute she did so, Ben reached out and touched it, a reverent look in his green eyes.

"Cool." He finally released the guitar pick so that it fell back against Sophie's neck, and then he grinned at her. "Anyway, I suppose I'd better go and try to sweet-talk Gerrard, but thanks for the luck." Then without another word he loped off down the corridor, leaving Sophie and her friends to stare at one another.

Finally, Kara spoke. "Okay, so can I just say that sixth grade is weird? I mean, did you ever in a million years think that Ben Griggs would ever come up and want to talk to the likes of us? And is it just me, or did he seem to think that Eddie Henry's guitar pick is magic or something."

"I know, he did, didn't he," Sophie agreed. "Which is crazy. It's just a guitar pick. How could it be magic?"

Harvey stared at them both for a moment before rolling his eyes. "Yeah, how dumb of a crazed pyromaniac to think that a guitar pick is magic. I mean, it's not like it's a sparkly apple-shaped ring or anything."

"Hey, that's different." Sophie immediately touched her djinn ring. "For a start, it's not like I think it brings me luck or anything. It is more just a channel for my djinn power. I mean, I don't even need to wear it anymore for my magic to work."

"But all the same, it might be worth asking Malik about the guitar pick," Kara advised. "Just in case the pick somehow got some weird mojo and Sophie gets another case of RWD by wearing it."

Sophie shuddered. When she had first started wearing her djinn ring, she had gone a bit overboard on the magic and had developed Random Wish Disorder. Technically, it was like chicken pox and not something she could get again, but it was probably best not to take any chances. "You're right, I'll ask him."

"And speaking of Malik, where is he?" Harvey suddenly started to glance around as he quickly shoved his half-eaten packet of M&M's back into his jacket pocket. "I hope he's not doing the invisible thing again, because I hate when he does that. Especially when I have snack foods."

"No, definitely no invisible thing—well, not in front of you guys anyway," Sophie assured him, since Malik could choose who could see and hear him and who couldn't. "But obviously he will be invisible to everyone else. Anyway, he said he would meet me here. It turns out that despite worshipping the ground my mom walks on, he refused to get in the car with us this morning. Apparently, he had a nasty run-in with a woman camel-train driver about a zillion years ago. I guess I should summon him just in case he's forgotten."

Sophie clapped her hands three times, and Malik suddenly appeared next to them. Today he was wearing some tight black jeans, a pair of pointy boots, and a white T-shirt, which was remarkably like what Zac had worn on his second day of school in the movie *17 Again*. Looks like he wasn't going to take her advice and change into anyone else.

"Greetings to you all." The djinn ghost did an elaborate bow and then shot them a dazzling smile. Harvey and Kara both blinked, but Malik didn't seem to notice as he glanced around the crowded corridor with a curious expression on his face. "Ah, so this is the famous Robert Robertson Middle School? Nice."

"Malik, you've been here loads of times," Sophie reminded him as she pulled the guitar pick out from under her adorably cute navy blouse and held it up to him. "Anyway, I wanted to know if you think this is magic."

"That thing?" Malik sniffed it for a moment before

he pulled an offended face. "Of course it's not magic. I mean, what self-respecting djinn would put his power into a junky old bit of plastic? Rule number one about being a djinn is that if you're going to put your magic into anything, you should make it something expensive. Preferably with sparkles on it. Actually, you should write that down."

"Junky?" Sophie slipped the guitar pick back under her shirt and looked at him with disgust. "This isn't junky. I'll have you know it belonged to the best bass player in the world. In fact, one just like it sold for over two hundred bucks on eBay. Not that I'd ever sell it, of course, but I'm just saying. It's not junky."

"Er, okay." Malik blinked before turning around, obviously bored with the conversation. "So anyway, what's up first? Should we do a group number? Or should I go straight to my solo? I'm thinking jazz hands."

Harvey turned to Sophie. "Um, what's he talking about?"

"*High School Musical*," Sophie reluctantly explained.

"As in the singing and dancing movie?" Harvey wrinkled his nose in distaste since the only movies he liked to watch were of the horror variety. The creepier the better.

"It's his new obsession," Kara added. "I guess he thinks that's what a regular school is like and that any second now we will just stop what we're doing and spontaneously break into song."

"Please, I'm not stupid," Malik protested with disdain. "I mean, of course it isn't *HSM*, as we call it in the biz. For a start, this is middle school, and obviously *Middle School Musical* just doesn't have the same pizzazz. Plus, I've got to say that the people here aren't nearly as good looking as Zac and Vanessa."

"That's because no one here is wearing makeup or spent three hours getting their hair done," Sophie said before she caught sight of Melissa Tait, who was still glaring at Sophie like she was something the cat dragged in (backward through a swamp). Sophie quickly amended. "Okay, so nearly no one here does that."

"Well, maybe they should consider it?" Malik pondered as he pulled out his camera phone and took a photograph of himself standing next to Sophie's locker.

"What are you doing?" Sophie was immediately distracted.

"It's for posterity," Malik explained. "Of course, it sucks that I'm a ghost, and so you can't actually see me in the shot, but it's still a good idea, is it not?" As he spoke he took another photograph of himself, this time giving a very cheesy thumbs-up, making him look more like a tourist than a two-thousand-year-old ex-djinn.

"It is not," Sophie asserted.

"Ha! You're such a joker," Malik said, undeterred as he studied the screen of the camera. Then he looked up and frowned. "And why do you keep looking over at the locker? If I didn't know better I would say that you're about to shape-shift into a giraffe the way your neck's stretching."

"I can shape-shift?" Sophie was immediately side-tracked. "I mean, I knew that you could, but I didn't think it was something that I could do. Why didn't you tell me? Perhaps I could do that for the Djinn Council instead of the transcendental conjuring? That might impress them even more."

"The reason I didn't tell you about it is because you've only got a very small brain and I didn't want it to get overloaded," Malik told her in a kindly voice. "Besides, I thought it would be better to master your borrowed powers first before concentrating on your internal ones."

"Borrowed powers? Internal powers? What are you talking about?"

"See, small brain," he said before sighing. "Fine. I'm talking about the fundamental elements of djinn magic. Borrowed powers are all the magic that comes through your djinn ring, and they're taken from everything around you—like the air, the trees, Harvey's M&M's. You use your borrowed powers for all the wishes that you do and for your transcendental conjurations.

"However, your internal powers are what are already inside you. For someone like Kara, it's nada, but for you, it's very strong. Probably because your father was Tariq the Awesome. Anyway, it's your internal power that allows you to do transfigurations. Now stop changing the subject and tell me why you keep looking at that locker. There isn't a purple ifrit in it, is there? Because if so, then you can tell him from me that I don't have the money. Furthermore, the Geneva Convention clearly states that when a djinn is under the influence of date juice and—"

"Malik there's no ifrit in there; it's just Jonathan Tait's locker," Kara interrupted in a gentle voice. "I think Sophie was hoping that she would see him before first period."

"No ifrit? Oh, boy. You gave me quite a scare there." Malik started to fan his face, but before he could say anything else the bell rang. Sophie and her friends wove their way through the throng of students toward their homeroom.

She was just biting back her disappointment at not seeing Jonathan when he suddenly bounded up next to her, an apologetic look on his face. Today he was dressed in an apple green Adidas hoodie and baggy jeans, his damp golden hair casually pushed back off his tanned forehead. Be still her beating heart.

"You're here." She grinned. "I wasn't sure if you were at school."

"I was trying to get in some last-minute basketball practice before Thursday's game," he explained as he shoved his hands into his back pockets. "But I didn't want you to think I was avoiding you. I mean, hanging out at our lockers has kind of become our thing."

Sophie grinned some more. First they'd had "a moment," and now they had "a thing"? Could this day get any more awesome?

"So how did it go? Are you all ready?" she forced

herself to ask so that she didn't look like a complete idiot.

"It went okay; it's the first game of the season, and it's my first game as captain, so I'm pretty nervous," he admitted before he suddenly took a deep breath and shot her a nervous glance. "I was hoping you might come along for good luck."

"Really? I would love to," Sophie instantly agreed before quickly adding, "Not that you need luck, of course, since you're an awesome basketball player."

"Thanks." A relieved smile tugged at his lips. "Especially since I know basketball isn't really your thing."

"Of course it is. I'm all about the basketball." She gave an enthusiastic nod before catching his surprised look. She let out a rueful sigh. "Well, okay, so perhaps playing it isn't really my thing, but I've got no problems watching it. Especially when you play. Oh, but I better not sit anywhere near your sister. I'm pretty sure she hates me. She gave me the look of death before."

"Of course she doesn't hate you," Jonathan assured her. "She just has problems flexing her facial muscles. Don't take it personally."

"Really? Because she looked pretty angry to me. Do you think it's still the jeans thing? I've seriously said sorry like a zillion times about that."

"Which is probably a zillion more than you needed to. Look, don't worry about Melissa. That's just the way she is, and until my parents will authorize the frontal lobotomy that I requested for her, we've just got to put up with it the best we can. Anyway, before I go, did you like the playlist I made you?"

"Totally." Sophie nodded as she felt another goofy smile coming up to her lips. At the concert, Jonathan had given her a CD full of his favorite songs, and she had been listening to them on her iPod ever since.

"Cool." He grinned back at her before letting out a reluctant sigh. "Well, I suppose I'd better go before I'm late, but I'll catch you later."

Sophie continued to smile as she watched him jog back up the empty corridor. Then she turned and walked into her homeroom. Malik was standing in front of Harvey and Kara and appeared to be demonstrating some hip-hop moves, but she hardly noticed as she started to hum one of the songs from Jonathan's playlist. First she'd had the good news about going to see the Djinn Council and finding out more about her dad's disappearance, and now she had Jonathan asking her to watch him play basketball. It was everything that a positive thinker like herself could ask for.

5

"OKAY, SO I KNOW I SAID THAT MALIK COULD COME to art class with me, but I swear that's an experience that I never want to repeat again," Kara announced as she collapsed at the cafeteria table next to Harvey, who was cramming food into his mouth and trying to read a textbook at the same time. Sophie, who had been discreetly listening to the playlist that Jonathan had made for her, pulled out her earbud and looked up.

"What happened? Was he terrible?" she cautiously asked as she nibbled on a chip. Not that she held out much hope for Malik's behavior since he had spent most of the morning being anything but okay. Then Sophie glanced around the table. "And more importantly, where is he now?"

"Just look for the orange ghost who's stealing Jell-O," Kara said as she pulled out the large sketch pad that never left her side and buried her head behind it. Sophie peered toward the long line at the food counter, where a very orange Malik was hovering over someone's lunch tray.

"You painted him?" Harvey finally looked up from the pasta he had been shoveling into his mouth.

"I didn't want to," Kara wailed from somewhere behind her sketch pad. "But he wore me down. He's like Chinese water torture. Drip, drip, drip. It was either paint him orange or have my cubist sketch look like something Jackson Pollock's cat would do. Besides, he promised me that once the paint hit him, it would be invisible to anyone who couldn't already see him." Kara cautiously peered over the sketch pad at Sophie. "Are you mad?"

"Of course not." Sophie shook her head and pulled the sketch pad down so she could clearly see her friend. "You don't have to tell me how annoying he is. Why do you think I conjure him up so many Cheetos? It's so I can keep him quiet. Besides, I appreciate your taking him. After the way he behaved in Spanish, I'm surprised that Señor Rena didn't give me a detention."

For a moment they were all quiet, as if individually remembering how Malik had started making Sophie's entire pencil case float in the air like it was possessed. He had even made sound effects, which, judging by the looks people had given them, could be clearly heard by everyone. The annoying thing was that when Sophie had asked him to put off potential house buyers by pretending her house was haunted, Malik had acted like he didn't have a clue as to what she was talking about.

Finally, Kara spoke. "So how long do you think he'll need to stay at school with us? Because we haven't even lasted half a day yet, and I'm already exhausted. I don't dare take him back to the art room again since he seemed to think that Colin the winged monkey was some kind of evil demon, and he kept throwing things at it. Now I'm going to have to redo one of the wings because Malik broke it."

"Oh, Kara," Sophie groaned. "I'm so sorry about Colin's wing. I had really hoped Malik would behave himself. But until I get my new appointment with the Djinn Council, I need him to keep training me. We just need to stay positive and think happy thoughts. Pretend that he's like a puppy."

"Puppies? Ewh, why are you talking about those hideous creatures?" Malik suddenly appeared next to them, his painted orange face smeared with red Jell-O, making him look like pumpkin roadkill. "By the way, have you tried this stuff? It's like pond scum but with sugar." As he spoke he lifted his black leather jacket from where it was draped over his arm to reveal a plate that was stacked with yet more fluorescent Jell-O, all violently wobbling, as if it knew what was coming next.

Why did Sophie get the feeling he hadn't paid for it either? But before she could say anything, Ben Griggs walked up to the table and gave her two thumbs up before pointing to the guitar pick around her neck. Sophie could only assume that he meant he had managed to convince Principal Gerrard not to give him a detention. She gave him a halfhearted wave in return and tried to ignore the triple strength, venomous glare that Melissa was throwing down from just behind him.

"Whoa, what was that about?" Kara blinked as the two seventh graders walked over to one of the popular tables. "Did you see the way she was looking at you?"

"I know, it was pretty magnificent." Malik whistled in appreciation. "That girl has serious spunk. I'm thinking that she could definitely play Sharpay in *High School Musical.* I bet she wouldn't even need to rehearse."

"That's because she's evil," Kara informed him before turning back to Sophie. "So, do you think it's still because of the jeans?"

Before she could answer, Harvey pushed away his half-eaten lunch. Both girls were immediately distracted since the number of times that Harvey didn't finish his lunch was never.

"Are you feeling okay?" Sophie forgot all about Melissa Tait and studied Harvey's face in concern.

"Yeah, I'm just freaking out about this stupid assignment. I'm going back to the library after school to work on it. Not that I'll get it finished by tomorrow."

"Of course you will." Sophie gave him an encouraging nod. "You just need to tell yourself that you can do this. Repeat after me: I'm a clever, well-rounded guy who's going to nail his history assignment and—"

"Soph," Harvey cut her off in a dry voice. "It's not going to work."

"Yes, it is," Sophie insisted as she reached over and

grabbed the notebook from his hand. She flicked it open to see what he'd done so far. The page was blank.

"I know," he groaned before she could say anything. "I tried to do it last night, but my dad took me to the apartment he's thinking of moving into. The spare bedroom is about the size of a bathroom and so are the cockroaches that are living there. It was kind of hard to concentrate after that."

Kara's large brown eyes immediately filled with sympathy. "H, that sucks so much. Why didn't you IM us about it?"

"Because it would've interfered with my denial process," Harvey explained. "Right now I need to use all of my energy not to think about it."

"Well, at least we can help with the assignment," Sophie assured him. "We can all go to the library after school. I can wish up all the textbooks you need so that you can do your research. Then tonight you can type it up and make it look all nice and shiny to hand in tomorrow morning."

Harvey shook his head so that his long bangs fell across his eyes. "You don't have to. It's not your fault I suck at history."

"Of course we're going to come with you," Kara said as the bell rang. Her friends got to their feet, and Sophie was just about to follow them when she caught sight of Miss Carson and Señor Rena standing by the front cafeteria door, glaring at her. Sophie gulped. Perhaps when she got better at transcendental conjuring, she could move them out of the way. Or, even better, she could turn herself invisible like Malik did. But for now it was probably better just to avoid them. She turned to her friends.

"You guys go ahead to English. I'm going to go the long way around."

"We'll go with you," Kara said as she followed Sophie's gaze over to where the teachers were still standing. But Harvey, who didn't like walking any farther than he had to unless food was involved, didn't look impressed.

Sophie quickly shook her head. "It's fine. I'll see you in a few minutes. Save me a seat."

Once her friends headed for the front entrance, Sophie began to thread her way through the tables toward the small door at the back of the cafeteria.

"So, about this library business after school. That doesn't include me, right?" Malik asked as he floated just above her head. "Because it sounds kind of dull. Besides, I have a much better idea. When I was with Kara in her art class, I saw a flyer for the school production. Did you know that the auditions are Thursday? Anyway, I thought I could go and get in some practice after school."

"What?" Sophie blinked at him.

"*The Wizard of Oz*. It's a musical," Malik explained in a patient voice. "Of course, I've got no idea why the wicked witch is green when everyone knows witches are purple. And the magic that they use in it is illogical, but really those are minor points."

"I know what *The Wizard of Oz* is, but I'm not sure why you want to practice when you can't audition. Anyway, I promised Harvey that we would help him, and since I can't trust you to stay out of trouble, you're coming with us."

"Fine," the djinn ghost grumbled. "But if I die of boredom, don't blame me."

"I wouldn't dream of it," Sophie replied as Malik sulkily floated ahead of her muttering something about "being bound all over again."

"Hey, come back here. Malik—"

"Who's Malik?" a voice replied, and Sophie looked up to see that Melissa Tait had fallen into step next to her. Her glossy blonde hair was hanging in perfect cascades down around her shoulders, and her outfit was straight out of the pages of *Teen Vogue*, with that kind of fashion-forward styling that Sophie would never have. Also, as usual, she looked like she'd just eaten a whole bag of sour gummi worms.

"Er, it's the lyrics from a song...Neanderthal Joe's new one," Sophie improvised as she realized that once again she had been caught talking to an invisible ghost (who for the record had now disappeared out of the cafeteria).

"No wonder I haven't heard it." Melissa gave a dismissive shrug before coming to a halt and folding her arms in front of her chest. "Don't think I don't see what you're doing."

"W-what am I doing?" Sophie resisted the urge to

lick her lips, since Harvey had once told her that was a sure giveaway of nerves. And it wasn't that she felt nervous around Melissa (because, really, *terrified* would be a much better word to sum up the situation). It was just that she didn't want to annoy Jonathan's twin sister more than she'd already managed to. "If this is about the jeans incident, then I've already told you how sorry I am. It was a complete accident. Plus, I replaced them for you. I'm not sure what else I can do."

"This isn't about the jeans," Melissa said in a frosty tone that, if applied correctly, could probably help keep the polar ice caps from melting for about the next gazillion years. "Though don't think I've forgotten about that, you freak."

"Oh, right." Sophie let out a sigh of relief before realizing that, if it wasn't about the jeans, it must be about something else. She took a deep breath and tried to think positive, happy thoughts as she cautiously said. "So what's the problem then?"

"I'll tell you what the problem is," Melissa said in a low voice. "It's you. Everywhere I look, there you are. First you're hanging all over my brother like some kind of barnacle. Going to concerts with him and doing stupid little wavy things at him from your locker. And now you're trying to get your stinky, unfiled nails into my boyfriend."

"What?" Sophie almost rubbed her ears to make sure she was hearing correctly. "You think I'm trying to steal your boyfriend?"

"*Trying* being the operative word there." Melissa gave an inelegant snort. "I mean, I know you're no threat, but for some stupid reason he thinks that revolting piece of plastic that you insist on wearing around your neck is a lucky charm."

"Yes, but that's not my fault," Sophie yelped. "And besides—"

"Do I look like I care what you have to say?" Melissa cut her off before narrowing her eyes (honestly, she must practice in the mirror or something). "I'm just warning you that you'd better stay away from Ben. Oh, and while you're at it, you can stay away from my brother, too. Do I make myself clear?" Then, without waiting for an answer, she sauntered off to where her look-alike best friends (Harvey liked to call them "the Tait-bots") were waiting for her.

Sophie gulped. Out of all the things she had thought Melissa might be annoyed about, she certainly hadn't guessed that. The only problem was, despite what Jonathan said, she knew that no good could come from Melissa Tait's trying to wage a vendetta against her. Which meant that if Sophie was going to have a perfect life, she would need to figure out a way to make peace with Jonathan's (evil) sister. Luckily, she had magic on her side.

AS WELL AS BEING A VERY POSITIVE PERSON, SOPHIE
was also a planner. Her dad had often told her that everything was easier when you had a good plan. However,
despite spending her last two classes trying to come up
with ways to stop Melissa Tait from hating her, she still
had nothing. She let out a frustrated sigh, put her blank
list into her backpack, and pushed her way to her locker.
As she did so she caught sight of Jonathan Tait.

He was on the other side of the hallway with a sea
of kids separating them, but the minute he saw her, he
looked up and smiled. Sophie immediately put her hand
up to her own so-straight-you-could-rule-lines-with-it
hair and made a quick wish so that it suddenly had a bit
more bounce and body. Then, once she felt it fluff up under her fingers, she returned his wave.

He held up a basketball as if to explain that he couldn't
talk to her right now. Sophie gave him a goofy smile and
then watched as he disappeared back into the crowd.

"Aww, that's so cute." Malik suddenly appeared next

to her. "But seriously, can I please go now? Because if I have to stay in this cursed place for one moment longer, then I'm pretty sure my brains will leak out all over the floor into a messy, slippery puddle, and innocent children might get hurt in the process. We must think of their safety."

"Do you think there's any chance at all that you might be exaggerating?" Sophie said as she dumped her books off and shut her locker.

"No." Malik gave an adamant shake of his head. "I can assure you that I'm underselling the situation, because seriously I had no idea that school could be so boring. So here's the deal, if you let me leave now, I could probably still catch an early show of *The Wizard of Oz* to listen to "Somewhere Over the Rainbow." Then when I've got my va-va-voom back, we can do some more work on your transcendental conjuring."

"Is he still trying to leave so that he and Eric can watch a touring production of *The Wizard of Oz*?" Kara asked as she and Harvey joined Sophie at her locker and the three of them headed toward the library. Sophie nodded her head.

"Yes, but it's not going to work since the last time he met up with Eric the Giant, he didn't come back for three days," Sophie said as they reached the library and made their way over to the beanbags in the corner. As soon as they got there, she wished for some easy-to-understand history books, and a moment later a neat stack of books appeared. Harvey reluctantly picked up one, but Malik just looked at them in disgust and floated to the top of one of the stacks.

"So how's it going with your Melissa Tait plan? Do you have any ideas?" Kara asked as they settled themselves down. Sophie shook her head and didn't bother to open the history book she was holding.

"What's this?" Malik immediately floated back down from the stacks, his sulky expression leaving his face, since the only thing he seemed to like more than Cheetos was gossip.

"I had a little run-in with Melissa Tait after you left the cafeteria, and it turns out that the reason she hates me is because she thinks that I'm trying to steal her boy-friend."

"'Ben Griggs?" Malik raised an eyebrow. "I would've thought he was way out of your league. I mean, I guess you're cute in the short-blonde-girl-next-door sort of way, but you're not really on Melissa's and Ben's level."

"Not to mention the fact he's a pyro, and according to Harvey, he likes to beat up sixth graders. Not exactly my type. Unfortunately, Melissa doesn't believe me. Oh, and she heard me talking to you before—well, I thought I was talking to you, but you weren't there—so now she thinks I'm crazy, too."

"Ouch." Malik winced. "If there was one person in this

whole entire nightmare of a school whom I wouldn't want as my enemy, Melissa Tait would be that girl. You should really try to fix that."

"That's what I'm trying to do," Sophie assured him. "But considering we don't have anything in common apart from Jonathan, it's not easy."

"I'll say," Kara agreed. "I mean, she's a cheerleader and you're not. She's in seventh grade and you're not. She's a normal nondjinn and you're not.... Oh. I've got it!"

"You do?" Sophie asked eagerly since she didn't like where Kara's speech had been going. "What is it?"

"Burnt sienna." Kara grinned before seeming to realize that Sophie was staring blankly at her. "It's a really gorgeous warm brown color. Anyway, you have a really cute T-shirt in that color, and the other day Melissa had the exact same color on the scarf she had tied around her purse. Anyway, you could talk about that. It might break the ice."

"Oh." Sophie blinked, not quite able to share her friend's enthusiasm. Then she brightened. "Or I could use my magic to conjure her up something in that color. That might work."

"Would that be ethical?" Kara pondered.

"I'll tell you what's not ethical," Harvey suddenly interrupted as he waved one of the books Sophie had conjured up for him. "It's making innocent kids have to read this stuff, because seriously, none of it makes sense. I mean, why did World War I start in France and Germany if it was the Archduke of Austria who was killed?"

"Archduke of Austria? Let me see that." As he spoke, Malik floated closer so that he was leaning over Harvey's shoulder. Then he made a clicking noise. "Well, of all the cover-ups in all the world. How can they say that it was because of simmering tensions? Please, the real reason that war started was because of Moroccan almonds. Seriously, Wilhelm II loved Moroccan almonds, and the French controlled the trade in Morocco and refused to let him buy any. We all tried to warn Poincaré that no good could come from standing in between Wilhelm and his almonds, but would he listen?"

Sophie, Kara, and Harvey all blinked simultaneously.

"Why are you looking at me like that?" Malik demanded. "It's true, and if you've ever tasted Moroccan almonds, you would understand."

"Right. Of course it is." Sophie nodded while trying not to smile. However, next to her Harvey wasn't looking quite as happy.

"Well, nuts or not, none of it is good. I'm about to become a product of a broken marriage. I can't afford to be a middle school dropout, too."

"You're not going to be a dropout," Kara reassured him.

"Kara's right," Sophie added. "From now on there will be no mention of anything that isn't history related. Deal?"

"Really?" Harvey looked relieved as Sophie flipped open her history book and started to jot down some notes for him, pointing out the best place for him to start.

An hour later the look of panic had left Harvey's face, and he started to gather up his notes. It wasn't the best assignment in the world, but since he hadn't downloaded it off the Internet and it didn't contain anything from Wikipedia, he was probably still ahead of half the class. Even Sophie had managed to do enough research so that tonight she could zap up her own assignment and still have time to practice her transcendental conjuring.

They got to their feet and tried to ignore the pained expression Malik was wearing as they headed down the hallway. It was well after four o'clock, but despite the time there was a group of people huddled up outside the gym door.

"What's going on?" Sophie wrinkled her nose.

"I've got no idea." Kara shook her head so that her long hair went tumbling over her shoulders.

"It's probably the cheerleading sign-up sheet to find a replacement for Donna Anderson. She broke her leg on Monday, and they need someone else before the big game on Thursday," Harvey said.

"Um, excuse me?" Kara demanded, since Harvey wasn't known for his love of sport.

"I got stuck sitting next to Benny Masters yesterday," Harvey admitted. "And he was telling me all about it— despite all the nonverbal cues I gave him to let him know I wasn't interested. Anyway, unless Sophie wants to have another Melissa run-in, we should probably go out the side door, because if there is one thing that girl loves more than herself, it's cheerleading."

"Good idea," Kara said. But instead of moving, Sophie stood where she was and widened her eyes.

"Harvey Trenton, you're a genius," she exclaimed as she clapped her hands together in excitement.

"I've often thought so," he agreed before looking confused. "Though I'm not sure what I just said to make you think that."

"You said that the one thing Melissa loves more than herself is cheerleading, so that's the perfect way for me to become friends with her."

Kara and Harvey looked at each other for a moment, as if hoping that the other one might understand what was going on before Harvey finally cleared his throat.

"Er, Soph," he said in a polite voice, "you do know that you're not a cheerleader, right?"

"I know, which is why it's so hard to make Melissa like me when we don't have anything in common. But imagine how much easier it would be if I was on the squad with her," Sophie explained, completely unable to contain her excitement at having the most perfect idea. Ever.

"Yes, but like Harvey just said, you're not a cheerleader," Kara repeated, still looking confused.

"Not yet," Sophie was forced to admit. "But thanks to some transcendental conjuring, I soon will be. Don't you see? It's the perfect way to practice my magic and win Melissa over all in one pom-pom-encrusted swoop."

"Can you even do that?" Harvey knitted his brows together. "I mean, the other day on the basketball court, it was pretty obvious that you were using magic. Are you sure you should be risking that all over again?"

"Yes, but that was before I started learning how to do all this new fancy stuff. I have much better powers of concentration now. Besides, it isn't going to be anything too big. Just a few twirls and high kicks," Sophie assured him before she turned to Malik. "So, is that something I can manage?"

"I guess so." Malik reluctantly nodded. "But remember that concentration is everything. If you lose focus and your wish goes awry, then you could find yourself in the middle of a crowded bazaar wearing only a piece of fabric that you had to steal from a blind beggar while all of your *supposed* friends laugh at a certain part of your anatomy in a very unkind way."

For a moment all three of them just stared at him before Sophie coughed. "Er, Malik, have you ever heard of the phrase 'too much information'?"

"Oh, right. Was that inappropriate?" he said, and Sophie nodded her head.

"A little bit," Kara told him in a kindhearted voice before turning back to Sophie, concern still covering her face. "Are you sure this is a good idea?"

"Of course I am." Sophie grinned. "And it just goes to prove how amazing the Universe is. I mean, I had a problem, and after doing some positive thinking, the most perfect solution suddenly landed in my lap. It would be wrong if I didn't follow it through." Then, without another word, she jogged over to the sign-up sheets and scribbled her name down. Had she mentioned that this was the best idea ever?

7

LATER THAT AFTERNOON SOPHIE REALIZED THAT there was one small kink in her perfect plan. Her bedroom. Not that there was anything wrong with her bedroom, apart from the fact that it wasn't designed to practice cheerleading routines in. Actually, it was a wonder she had never noticed before just how small it was. There was no way she could even attempt to do a high kick, let alone a magically induced backflip.

Of course, if Malik had been there, she could have asked him if there was a way around the problem, but he had stepped outside an hour ago to take a cell-phone call and she hadn't seen him since. No points for guessing that he and Eric the Giant were currently watching a production of *The Wizard of Oz* somewhere. Which meant she was going to have to figure this one out on her own.

She chewed her lip and was just trying to decide what to do when there was a knock on her door. A moment later her mom appeared.

"I just wanted to see how the history assignment's going," her mom said. As usual she was wearing one of Sophie's dad's old shirts, her straight blonde hair was tied up in a messy knot, and there was a smudge of clay on her nose.

"All done." Sophie held up the assignment that she'd zapped up earlier. Three weeks ago her mom would've just believed her, but thanks to a few ups and downs after her djinn magic had first come through, these days her mom wanted cold, hard evidence. If only her space problem was so easily solved. Then she realized her mom was still looking at her, and Sophie felt a stab of panic. "I-is everything okay?"

"Yes, everything's fine. Well, apart from the leak in my studio. I discovered it this morning and have spent most of the day moving my stock down into the basement in case it rains. Unfortunately, the basement's now full, so I was hoping you could move some of the old boxes of junk up to the garage for the thrift store to collect. I'm already so far behind on this order, and I really need to get it glazed this afternoon."

Sophie was about to make some excuse, since moving boxes from the basement was her least favorite job ever (not because she was trying to be unhelpful, but because for some reason known only to bug experts, there were about a zillion spiders in her basement, and not one of them was nice and friendly like Charlotte). However, she suddenly realized that despite its spider problem, the basement was actually the perfect place to do some magical cheerleading. And if she used her powers to move the boxes, she would have plenty of time to practice. Plus, after all the chaos Malik had been causing around the house lately, the very least Sophie could do was help out.

"Of course," she said as she followed her mom downstairs, while trying to ignore the fact that Meg was lounging around in front of the television, not even pretending that she was going to help.

The basement was just as dark and musty as Sophie remembered, but her mom didn't seem to notice as she led Sophie over to a huge pile of boxes that was sitting in the middle of the floor. Sophie flipped the lid on the first box and was greeted by a bag of marbles and Meg's old Barbie dolls, which all had bite marks on the legs. Then she caught sight of a hideous green sweater that she vaguely remembered loving when she was five years old. She turned to her mom.

"I didn't know we still had all of this stuff."

"I guess I should've sorted through everything sooner, but the idea of throwing away memories all seemed too difficult," her mom said as she opened up another box and held up a pair of flared jeans that looked like they'd walked straight out of the seventies.

"Really?" Sophie raised an eyebrow as she pulled out a long white T-shirt, which had a picture of a lion on the front of it. "It doesn't seem like it would be too hard."

"Hey, cheeky child, I will have you know that this was considered to be the height of fashion at the time," her mom protested as she studied the T-shirt for a moment before ruefully putting it back in the box and shutting the lid. "But it wasn't until I needed more space that I realized just how much junk we have down here. Besides, memories don't exist in clothes and possessions, they exist in our minds. So, will you be okay to carry the boxes up to the garage?"

"Of course," Sophie readily agreed, since she knew she had magic on her side.

She waited until her mom disappeared back upstairs before she turned her attention to the boxes. There were at least fifteen of them, and she closed her eyes and wished for all of them to move to the garage. A second later she felt a tingle go racing through her, and when she opened her eyes, the boxes were gone. Now she just had to check that they had actually turned up where they were meant to.

A couple of minutes later she was standing in the garage, grinning. Not bad for a few seconds of work. She couldn't help but think how great it would be if the Djinn Council wanted to test her box-moving skills. Still, she was sure that by the end of the afternoon she would be just as good at transcendental conjuring, and with that thought, she made her way back down to the basement and got to work.

An hour later Sophie stared at herself in the large mirror she had magically conjured up. Her transformation was amazing. She'd probably been eight years old the last time she'd attempted to do a high kick, and the result had been a bruised butt and some major embarrassment. But now all she had to do was visualize it in her mind and then her legs seemed to take on a life of their own. She held up her newly wished for pom-poms and decided to have one last practice.

"Gimme an M," she mouthed, before picturing herself doing a backflip. A second later her body leaned back and her spine formed a perfect arch before her legs kicked off the ground and came down on the other side of her head like she'd been doing it for years. Amazing! However, before she could attempt it again she heard the sound of footsteps coming down the stairs.

Sophie quickly wished for the large mirror and the pom-poms to disappear, just as her mom walked in. It was obvious by the smile on her face that she'd already seen the large pile of boxes and junk that Sophie had magically transported from the basement to the garage.

"I'm impressed. I didn't expect you would get so much done today," her mom said before she walked over to a second pile of things. "Perhaps we can start on this lot tomorrow."

"Sure," Sophie said as she started to head toward the stairs. But before she got there her mom coughed.

"By the way, is there something you want to tell me?"

Sophie froze as she realized perhaps she *hadn't* managed to get away with using so much magic after all.

"W-what do you mean?" she asked in a cautious voice as it suddenly occurred to her that perhaps Meg had been in the garage and had seen the boxes appearing from no-where.

"How about a certain daughter who put her name down for the cheerleading tryouts tomorrow?"

"Oh." Sophie gulped. "Did I forget to mention that?"

"Yes, you did." Her mom gave a dry cough as she stud-ied Sophie's face. "The school just rang to make sure that you bring along your permission slip. So how long have you been interested in cheerleading?"

"Well, you know, I've always found it fascinating." So-phie tried to make her voice sound casual.

"Really?" Her mom raised an eyebrow. "And this new interest wouldn't have anything to do with the fact that Jonathan is captain of the basketball team, would it? Be-cause, honey, you really shouldn't try to do anything spe-cial just to impress a boy."

Please. If she was going to do anything to impress Jonathan Tait, it would be along the lines of remembering all of the Ne-anderthal Joe tour dates for the last year, rather than trying to get onto a cheerleading team. "Okay, I'm doing it to try to become friends with Jonathan's sister, Melissa. The thing is, she hates me."

"I'm sure that's not true."

"Actually, it is," Sophie assured her. "She told me so herself. Have you ever had anyone hate you before?"

"Well, there was this time when my two daughters were pretty annoyed at me," her mom said in a serious voice before her brown eyes started to twinkle. *"Something about not wanting me to sell the family house..."*

"Ha-ha-ha, very funny. You know we didn't hate you. We just hated the idea of moving. Especially to Montana," she said, before pausing and peering back up at her mom. "So have you? Ever had someone hate you, I mean?"

Her mom chewed her lip for a moment and sat on the edge of an old suitcase. "Honestly, I don't know. Maybe they have and they just didn't mention it? But as someone who has done her fair share of hating, I can tell you that it's a pretty negative emotion."

"What? No way." Sophie gave a resolute shake of her head. "You won't even kill spiders. Not even the big ugly ones, and if you can't hate them, I refuse to believe that you could hate an actual person."

"I'm afraid it's true." Her mom gave her an embarrassed smile. "There was a time after your father left when I was sure I hated him. I still loved him, of course, but I was pretty angry, too. Actually, I was a lot angry."

"Oh." Sophie felt her heart ache since her mom didn't often talk about this kind of stuff.

"But the thing is," her mom continued, as she started to examine the hem of her shirt, "even though it took a while, I finally realized that I had to let go of the hate because it was eating me up. So I really don't think that you need to join the cheerleading squad just to get Melissa to like you. Why don't you just talk to her? Because I bet you'll find that if you push past the surface, deep down Melissa's actually just insecure and unhappy. I know I was."

Yes, and while that sounded good in theory, Sophie was pretty sure that if she pushed past the surface of Melissa Tait's evil exterior, all she would find would be more evil, probably wrapped up in some mega-trendy sweater that came from a store that Sophie had never even heard of. But before Sophie could say anything else, Meg stomped down the basement stairs holding the cordless phone, looking grumpy. She said there was a man called Alex on the phone.

"Alex is the builder, calling with a quote for the studio." Their mom immediately took the phone and shot Sophie a hopeful look. "Oh, there're a couple more boxes over there I forgot to ask you about. Would you mind moving them up to the garage, too?"

"Sure." Sophie nodded. Once her mom had disappeared back up the stairs, she headed toward the extra boxes. She was just about to magically wish them into the garage before she remembered that Meg was still standing there looking sulky. Instead, Sophie reluctantly picked up the first box. It weighed a ton, and she quickly wished for it to be light as a feather. Then she realized that Meg was still just standing there. "Er, I think you can help as well, thanks."

"Not likely. I'm not a traitor." Meg folded her arms and poked her bottom lip out.

"Since when am I a traitor for helping Mom?" Sophie demanded. "In fact, if anyone's a traitor, you are, since you've been having major tantrums. I thought we were trying to help her not stress out."

"Yeah, well, if you want to help Mom throw away Dad's boxes, then that's fine by me," Meg retorted before narrowing her eyes. *"Traitor."*

"What?" Sophie immediately dropped the box she had been holding. There was the sound of something breaking, but she ignored it as she turned to her sister. "Of course I'm not helping her throw out Dad's boxes."

However, Meg's mouth remained in a stubborn line, and Sophie suddenly felt a stab of panic go racing through her. She hadn't actually checked all the boxes her mom had told her to move. Instead, she had just magically zapped them up into the garage. Plus, despite the fact Meg was only six years old, she had an uncanny knack of always knowing what was going on. Sophie raced over to where her dad's boxes were kept. Relief flooded through her as she did a quick count. It looked like they were all there.

From time to time Sophie actually braved the spiders and came down to look at the cartons, hoping they might give her some answers about why he had left. Unfortunately, they never did, but she still couldn't bear the idea of their not being there. Several of them were filled with his clothes, apart from the ones her mom pilfered for her pottery smocks, but Sophie's favorite ones were the boxes with his cooking things. He had been a great cook, and not only did he have a huge collection of recipe books but there was also box after box filled with stainless steel bowls and packets of herbs that neither Sophie nor her mom had a clue what to do with.

Sophie turned back to Meg. "See. I told you I didn't move them. Why would you even think that?"

"Because when Jessica Dalton—who I hate more than anything—was looking for me before, I went and hid in Mom's studio. That's when I heard her on the telephone telling someone that she needed to make more room in the basement for her pottery. She said that she was going to get rid of some old stuff because it was time to move on."

"Yes, well, that just proves no good ever comes from eavesdropping, because the only things that Mom wanted me to move were some boxes of old clothes and toys," Sophie retorted, as she put her hands on Meg's shoulders and steered her back to the stairs. "And speaking of which, Mom would flip out if she knew that you had been eavesdropping on her."

However, instead of looking contrite, Meg just wriggled out of Sophie's grip and stomped through the kitchen and back to her room. Sophie's mom, who was no longer on the phone, widened her eyes in surprise.

"What was *that* about?"

Sophie just shook her head; despite her threat, she

wouldn't really tell on her sister. "You don't want to know, but trust me, the sooner Meg makes up with Jessica Dalton, the better."

"Tell me about it," her mom agreed. "She's been like a bear with a sore head. Oh, and by the way, Kara rang while I was on the phone. I said you'd call her back."

Sophie immediately forgot about her moody little sister as she grabbed the phone and disappeared into the privacy of her room to tell Kara how her training session had gone.

The next morning Sophie was brimming with happiness. She'd done a bit more transcendental conjuring last night in her room and had successfully managed to make Mr. Pugsy not just fly but also do backflips and twirls. Plus, she'd had a really great IM chat with Jonathan Tait, during which they'd reenacted the entire Neanderthal Joe concert, complete with a play-by-play of Eddie Henry giving her the guitar pick. The only slight worry was that Malik hadn't reappeared yet, but she was sure he'd be back soon.

She made her way down to the kitchen, where Meg was sitting at the table staring at a bowl of oatmeal, her arms firmly crossed in front of her.

"You haven't even touched it," her mom was saying.

"That's because it's gray and sludgy," Meg retorted as she unfolded her arms and pushed the bowl away. "Jessica Dalton's mom never makes her eat gray, sludgy stuff."

"Yes, and Mrs. Dalton never makes you eat it either,"

their mom pointed out in a serene voice. "But since Jessica asked you over for breakfast this morning and you wouldn't even answer her, you're stuck with my oatmeal."

"I didn't answer her because I'm never speaking to her again," Meg clarified in a menacing voice. "I hate Jessica Dalton, and—"

"And I really need to get to school," Sophie interrupted, since she didn't want a repeat of Meg's grumpy mood. She hurried over and gave her mom a kiss on the cheek. "So I will see you both later."

"Hey, not so fast." Her mom put down the pot of oatmeal (which Sophie had thankfully managed to avoid by going down earlier and making herself some toast) and turned to Sophie with a concerned expression on her face. "Before you go, I do have another favor to ask."

At the mention of that Meg stiffened, and even Sophie caught her breath for half a moment in case there had been something to what Meg had said. "It's not more box moving, is it?"

"No," her mom assured her, but before Sophie could give Meg a "told you so" look, Malik suddenly appeared in the kitchen. Today he was wearing an I'M WICKED T-shirt, pink sunglasses, and a gold medallion around his neck. No guesses for where he had been all this time. Sophie winced before realizing her mom was still looking at her.

"Er, so what is the favor then?"

"I was hoping you could look after Meg this afternoon. Max Rivers wants me to go and see him. He's thinking of selling some of my pottery in the store. Isn't that fantastic?"

"What?" Sophie yelped. She wasn't a fan of babysitting Meg at the best of times, let alone while she was so grumpy. Not to mention the fact that she wanted to get Malik out of the kitchen as quickly as she could. "The thing is—" she started to explain, but before she could finish Malik suddenly cut her off.

"Max? Huh, so why do I know that name?" The djinn toyed with his gold medallion for a moment before widening his eyes. "Hey, isn't he the guy who had the bottle I was trapped in? Because, while I know he had nothing to do with my binding, I can't help but think he's not a nice guy. You should tell your mom not to have anything to do with him."

Sophie, who was used to Malik's talking, despite the fact that her mom and Meg couldn't see him, just ignored what he was saying. But Mr. Jaws started to hiss from over by the window seat.

"Actually," Malik continued to muse as he floated over to where the cordless telephone was kept, "I think I should take his number out of your mom's book so that she won't be tempted to call him. Kind of like an intervention."

"Don't you dare!" Sophie yelped out loud before she could stop herself. However, despite the strange look her mom was giving her, Sophie knew it would get only stranger if Malik picked up the address book, since to her mom and Meg it would look like it was disappearing into thin air. Sophie lunged for the book and just beat Malik to it. At the same time Mr. Jaws leaped into action and came sliding across the hardwood floor and hissed at them both.

"Don't dare what? Are you okay?" her mom asked in alarm. Sophie hugged the book close to her chest and tried to ignore Mr. Jaws, who was now attacking her leg like she was some kind of deranged monster.

"Um, yes. I'm fine," Sophie said as she looked at the address book in her hands and tried to shake the cat off her leg. "I just meant…er, don't you dare think that you need to call up a sitter, because I would love to babysit Meg. Yup, count me in."

"Well, if you're going to babysit me, then you have to play three games of shark and watch two documentaries," Meg immediately dictated. "And I'm *not* going anywhere near the basement."

"Fine. Three games of shark and two documentaries." Sophie gritted her teeth and shot Malik an annoyed glare. He was so going to get it later. Thankfully, her mom didn't seem to notice. Instead, she smiled.

"Oh, then that's settled. And good luck with the cheerleading. I'll look forward to hearing how it goes."

"Sure, yeah." Sophie nodded, but as soon as they were out of hearing, she turned to Malik and folded her arms. "What was *that* all about?"

"That was me trying to be helpful," Malik explained. "Since clearly your mom shouldn't have anything to do with a man who keeps sahir-tainted bottles in his basement. I mean, it's just common sense."

"Yes, well, thanks to you, I now have to spend the afternoon babysitting Meg instead of practicing my magic for the Djinn Council. Oh, and FYI, wherever Meg is, Mr. Jaws and his 'I hate you' hiss aren't far behind, which will make it even more painful. So what do you have to say to that, Mr. Helpful?"

"Okay, maybe I shouldn't have tried to pick up the address book," Malik conceded, before shooting her a confident smile. "But I hardly think you can say I'm not helpful. I'm the most helpful djinn guide in the world."

"Really? Because maybe you need a new definition of helpful."

"You know words can hurt," Malik reminded her with a pout. "When have I ever been anything less than helpful?"

"Well, let's see. You made Kara paint you orange, you stole Jell-O, and then you disappeared and went to see a musical when you were supposed to be helping me practice my transcendental conjuring. And that was just yesterday. As for the day before, if I recall, you made a huge mess in the dining room and stole my mom's pottery glaze. And then day before *that*—"

"Fine," Malik admitted. "I concede that *sometimes* I can slip up."

"Sometimes?" Sophie raised her eyebrows at him. "The thing is, Malik, I just wish that you would—"

"Whoa." Malik held his hand up in horror. "Hey! Careful how you bandy that word about. I've spent far too long being bound to evil sahirs. I don't want to be stuck taking commands from you just because you accidently said the *W* word."

"What?" Sophie looked at him blankly for a moment before widening her eyes. "Oh, sorry, I didn't actually mean I was going to say it. It was just a figure of speech. You know that, right?"

"Yes, well, it's one figure of speech that you need to get rid of pretty darn quickly," Malik assured her. "Because rule number one of being a djinn is *never to WISH that anything happens to your djinn guide.* You should probably write that down."

Sophie flushed. "I promise it won't happen again," she assured him, because while Malik definitely drove her crazy most of the time, she would never want to be responsible for binding him. Especially since he'd just recently escaped from being bound to a bottle for over two hundred years.

"Okay, I believe you." Malik sniffed. "And I suppose you do have a point. I'm the one who got you into this whole djinn business, and it's my responsibility to help you. So I promise that from now on you'll get nothing but help from me. Help, help, help. Starting with a phone call to my buddy on the council."

"You haven't done that yet?" Sophie yelped.

"Er, um, of course I have," Malik said, not quite returning her gaze. "But, you know, it wouldn't hurt for me to call him again. Oh, look, here are Kara and Harvey, which I'm telling you because I like to help."

"What's he talking about?" Harvey demanded. "And why is he pretending to pat my hair?"

"I'm not patting it, I'm smoothing it down," Malik corrected, even though as a ghost he couldn't actually touch Harvey's hair. "Because that's what helpful djinns do."

"It's a very long story," Sophie said as they made their way toward the bus stop and she tried to figure out if a helpful Malik was any better than an annoying one.

ONCE THEY REACHED SCHOOL, THEY ALL WENT
their separate ways: Kara and Malik hurried off to a
meeting with the stagehands, while Harvey was caught
up in an argument with Greg Coombs on whether *The
Shining* was the scariest movie ever made. Sophie watched
them go and then busied herself with her locker combina-
tion while really hoping that she would see Jonathan.

She had just finished shoving all of her books into her
locker when she caught sight of him. For a moment he
looked at her in surprise before jogging over. She paused
and wished that her hair was fabulous (because there was
positive thinking and there was flat hair, and she knew
what side she liked to be on). A second later she felt it
happen, and she gave her new, perkier hair a quick pat.

"Hey." Jonathan shot her a cautious look. "So I wasn't
sure if you were still talking to me."

"W-what do you mean?" Sophie looked at him in alarm
as she went through a mental list of all the possible things
that Malik might've done between her IM conversation

with Jonathan last night until now. It was a long list.

"Last night after I got off the computer with you, I totally busted Melissa talking to one of her stupid friends about how she'd read you the riot act because you were crushing on Ben. Is it true?"

Okay, she hadn't seen that one coming.

"What? No, of course it's not true," Sophie yelped. "Well, I mean, yes, it's true that Melissa yelled at me, but the stuff about me liking Ben? So far from the truth that it's not even funny." Then she paused and nervously peered up at him. "You believe me, don't you?"

"Of course I do. You're far too normal to like Ben," Jonathan instantly assured her before looking relieved. "I just feel bad that my stupid sister did that to you. She's so dramatic. I swear this is what comes from my parents letting her watch so much MTV. So are we cool?"

"Of course." She nodded her head the way Harvey had taught her to do when she wanted to positively reinforce something. "Don't even worry about it."

"Phew," Jonathan said, looking completely adorable. "And seriously, just try to ignore Melissa. She'll find someone else to torture soon enough. So I was thinking that since the big game is on Thursday, you might want to meet up for lunch today."

"Actually," Sophie winced, "I'm kind of busy today. I'm going to try out for the open spot in the cheerleading squad."

"Are you serious?" Now Jonathan's eyes were so wide

that Sophie thought they might pop out of his head, like in one of the horror movies that Harvey loved. Then he let out a long groan. "Please tell me that this doesn't have anything to do with my sister."

"Of course not," Sophie assured him before realizing he didn't look remotely convinced. "Okay, yes, it does. But I just figured that if I could find a way to be friends with her, it might make things a bit easier between us. Plus, as a positive person, I feel it's my duty to try to fix the situation. Hence the cheerleading."

Jonathan paused for a moment before shaking his head. "I really don't think that's such a good idea. You're better off just steering clear of her."

"It's too late now. I've already put my name down for the tryouts. I really think it will work," Sophie insisted.

Jonathan still didn't look convinced, but he merely shrugged.

"Okay, it's your call," he said in a low voice as his gorgeous eyes stared directly at her. Sophie felt her stomach flip in excitement. A girl could definitely get used to this. And she didn't even have to use any magic!

"Right, that's it for today." Sophie's history teacher clapped her hands and reminded everyone that now that they'd finished with World War I, it was time to start discussing some of the causes of World War II. Harvey made a groaning noise as he got to his feet, but Sophie hardly noticed since she was still grinning after her conversation with Jonathan. *Had she mentioned how intense his gaze was?*

"How can there be so many wars?" Harvey demanded. "Anyway, I hope one of you guys was taking notes because I was too busy losing the will to live."

"Sorry." Kara, who had been looking distracted all morning, shook her head, but before Sophie could say anything else, their history teacher walked over.

"Sophie, may I have a word with you before you go?"

"Oh, sure." Sophie nodded to her friends that she would catch up with them, and she made her way to the front of the classroom with Malik floating above her head and giving her what she could only assume was meant to be a helpful smile. She ignored him as she turned to her teacher. "Is something wrong?"

"Actually, it's about your assignment. I must say I was a little surprised when I started to read it. I know you've had a few problems with some of your teachers since you started here, but I've been nothing but impressed with your contribution to my class."

"Thank you," Sophie said as she wondered if this was some kind of sign that everything was going to be okay.

"Until now," her teacher added as she held up the assignment and shot Sophie a confused look. "Moroccan almonds were the cause of World War I? Is this some kind of joke?"

"W-what?" Sophie's jaw dropped in surprise before she realized that Malik was grinning at her. She instantly felt her Jonathan-induced good mood dissolve.

"See, I told you I could be helpful. And you don't even need to say thank you, because I did it out of the goodness of my heart," he explained before bowing with a flourish and disappearing from the room. Sophie made a mental note to kill him. And not in a nice way either.

"So?" her teacher said, oblivious to what Malik had been saying (or doing). "Do you have some kind of explanation?"

Of course she did. Unfortunately, she didn't think that her teacher would appreciate what it was, so she let out a reluctant sigh. "I-I did an extra assignment as a joke. I guess I picked up the wrong one off my desk."

Her teacher raised an eyebrow. "That's how you spend your spare time? Making up crazy alternative-history assignments?"

"Yup." Sophie forced herself to agree. "I'm wacky like that. Anyway, I'm sorry I handed in the wrong one."

"So are you saying that you have the correct assignment for me?"

"I certainly do." Sophie let out a sigh of relief before realizing that she couldn't very well conjure it up in front of the teacher. "But, er, it's at home. I can bring it in first thing tomorrow."

"I'm taking a group of seventh graders to the museum tomorrow, so I won't be here, but I will expect it on my desk first thing on Friday morning. And I don't want anything like this to happen again. Are we clear?"

"Absolutely. It will be on your desk on Friday morning," Sophie solemnly promised. The minute her teacher nodded her head to the door, Sophie gratefully darted out to where Kara and Harvey were waiting for her.

"Please tell me that I didn't just hear Moroccan almonds," Kara yelped.

"I'm afraid so. Apparently, Malik thought he was being helpful."

"I *was* being helpful," Malik corrected as his Zac head appeared from the wall and then the rest of his body followed him. "And if you would like me to talk to this teacher of yours about what really happened back then, I would be happy to do so. Even if she is a spitter."

"Absolutely not." Sophie shook her head in alarm. "No talking to anyone, especially not my teachers. And no more changing my schoolwork. You have no idea how annoyed she was. I had to tell her it was a joke."

"I hardly think that World War I was a laughing matter," Malik said in a pious voice. "Now the cold war, on the other hand, actually did start out as a joke. You see, what happened was—"

"Malik." Sophie shook her head. "Seriously, no more alternative-history lessons. You're not helping. I don't understand how you even saw my assignment."

"Oh, it was on your desk this morning, and I realized how many mistakes you had in it. So I thought I would give you a helping hand—though I see now that I was mistaken," he quickly added as he caught the pained expression on Sophie's face. "Anyway, it's over now, and as long as you conjure up a new one by Friday there's no harm done."

"I guess," Sophie was forced to concede.

"And," Malik added with a dramatic flourish of his hands, "I also spoke to my friend at the Djinn Council, so hopefully you should get a new appointment delivered to you very soon."

"Really?" Sophie was instantly distracted, and she gave him a grateful smile. "Thank you. I really appreciate it. Anyway, I suppose we'd better get to the tryouts now."

"Actually," Kara mumbled in a small voice, her eyes fixed firmly on the ground, "please don't hate me, but at the meeting this morning I found out *The Wizard of Oz* auditions have been changed to today. I mean, I don't have to go, but I did say I would. And the thing is that—"

"I knew there was something weird going on with you!" Harvey announced. "You've been fiddling with your pencil all morning. I should've guessed it was something like this."

"Kara, why didn't you say something earlier?" Sophie immediately felt guilty that she'd been so caught up in her own Jonathan-Tait-stared-at-me happiness that she hadn't even noticed her friend had been worried about something.

"Because I didn't want to stress you," Kara said. "Besides, it's no big deal."

"Of course it's a big deal. You've been working on Colin the winged monkey statue nonstop. It's only right you should be at the auditions," Sophie quickly assured her. Unfortunately, Malik didn't seem to be taking the news quite so well.

"What?" he yelped, his Zac-like face drained of color. "They can't do that. The pamphlet clearly says that the auditions are tomorrow. I mean, what's the point of putting down a time if they're going to change it? This is very unprofessional."

"I know," Kara said. "But there was some kind of double booking going on, and they had to make the switch. I'm so sorry."

"Well, I should think so. I mean, this is a disaster. How can I go to *The Wizard of Oz* auditions *and* the cheerleading tryouts at the same time? I feel so torn."

"I wasn't actually apologizing to you," Kara said in surprise. "I was apologizing to Sophie."

"Why? Sophie isn't the one who wants to do two things at once," Malik snapped as he began to fan himself. "Do you think this is how Zac felt when they tried to make him choose between basketball and the musical?"

"Well, let's see. Zac was playing a character in a movie, and you're a djinn ghost who can't actually try out for either thing, so, yes, it's exactly the same," Harvey said in a dry voice.

"Do you think this is funny?" Malik demanded as he shot him a withering glare. "I mean, I really wanted to see *The Wizard of Oz* auditions. I've been listening to some of them practice, and it's like all the losers from *American Idol* rolled into one. Oh, this is a total disaster. What am I going to do?"

"You're going to the cheerleading tryouts with Sophie," Kara informed him in a firm voice. "I mean, you're her djinn guide, and she's about to do some seriously hard conjuring."

"Yes," Harvey added. "It would be the *helpful* thing to do."

Malik let out a long heartfelt sigh as his shoulders drooped. "I suppose you're right. And perhaps Zac Efron will be there? I mean, the basketball players seemed tight with the cheerleaders."

"I'm pretty sure that he won't be," Sophie assured him before studying Malik's face for a moment. "And perhaps it would be best if you did go to *The Wizard of Oz* auditions."

"Really?" Malik immediately perked up.

Harvey turned to Sophie and frowned. "And are you really sure about this?"

"Yes," Sophie assured him, secretly relieved that the troublesome djinn would be occupied for an hour. "Besides, I nailed it when I was rehearsing my transcendental conjuring in the basement, and Malik wasn't there then. I'll be fine."

"That's the spirit." Malik applauded her. "Just don't forget to hold your stomach in and stay focused. Oh, and remember what I said about clicking your fingers. It will definitely give it a bit of pizzazz," he said, before clicking his own fingers and disappearing from sight. Kara gave Sophie a tight hug and wished her luck before she headed toward the auditorium.

Once they were gone, it didn't take long for Sophie to change into her PE gear, and before she knew it, she and Harvey were racing toward the gymnasium. Okay, so she was racing and Harvey was halfheartedly tagging along. When they reached the gymnasium door, she turned to him and gave him a grateful smile.

"Thanks for coming with me. I know you think that I'm crazy, but I really don't think the Universe would've given me this idea if I wasn't meant to do it. Plus, according to Malik, the Djinn Council members are totally scary, so I figure facing down Melissa Tait will be good practice."

"It's okay, Soph." Harvey squeezed her hand. "I get why you want to patch this mess up, and since I once tried writing a poem to my mom and pretended it was from my dad, it would be wrong of me to call any of your ideas crazy."

"Thanks, Harvey." Sophie once again realized how lucky she was to have such amazing friends, especially when they had problems of their own going on. "You really are the best."

"I know," he said with a smile. "Now go and do your thing. But watch out if Melissa folds her arms, because in body-language talk, that's a declaration of war," he warned, just as his stomach made a growling noise in protest at having missed lunch. Without thinking, Sophie closed her eyes and made a wish. The next second a surprised-looking Harvey was holding a supersize Big Mac combo.

He widened his eyes in appreciation. Sophie grinned. She was in such a good mood that she couldn't help but make sure everyone else felt as happy as she did. Then she pushed open the gym door and glanced around her.

The sound of sneakers squeaking against the wood assaulted her ears, as hopeful cheerleaders were high kicking and spelling things at the same time. Over in the corner the members of the squad were standing around watching (except for Donna Anderson, who sat on a bench with her leg covered in a huge cast, looking miserable).

For a moment Sophie shuddered. Normally, she would rather poke herself in the eye with one of Kara's sketching pencils than spend time in this kind of environment, but extreme circumstances called for extreme measures.

She took a deep breath and was just about to head over when Ben Griggs suddenly appeared next to her. "Hey, Campbell, there you are. I'm totally stressing about my Spanish quiz this afternoon. If I don't pass it, I won't be able to play in the game tomorrow. I was wondering if I could touch the guitar pick again to give me some good luck. My old man will hit the roof if I get benched."

What? Sophie gulped. Letting Ben Griggs touch her

guitar pick had already caused far too many problems with Melissa. "The thing is—" she started, but Ben cut her off.

"Please, I really need you to help me out here. Come on, Campbell," he wheedled.

Sophie stifled a groan as she remembered her new affirmation. *I am a kind and friendly person who gets along with everyone.* Against her better judgment she had to admit that it wasn't very kind or friendly to say no to Ben when he was freaking out. She reluctantly pulled the necklace out from under her T-shirt.

"Fine, but be quick. I've got to go join the rest of the cheerleaders."

"Totally," Ben agreed as he reached out and clutched the guitar pick like it was some kind of holy grail. Sophie was just wondering how long he was going to take when she glanced over to the bleachers and caught sight of Harvey making weird faces at her.

She wrinkled her nose. Was he trying to remind her that Ben Griggs was a pyromaniac who liked to beat up on sixth graders? Because, hello, she already knew that. She raised her eyebrows at him, but instead of stopping, he began a series of hand actions. She really must ask Malik about whether her djinn powers could extend to mind reading, because this was making no sense at all.

"Well, well. Isn't this nice and cozy," Melissa Tait's voice suddenly rang out from somewhere behind Sophie's shoulder. Too late she figured out what her friend had been trying to tell her. For a moment she looked over to where Harvey was staring helplessly at her from the bleachers, before she slowly turned around to face her nemesis. Somehow, she didn't think her new affirmation was going to help much.

OH, HEY, BABE. I WAS JUST GETTING SOME GOOD luck for my Spanish quiz. There's no way I'll get benched for tomorrow's game now." Ben let go of the guitar pick.

"Of course you'll pass it," Melissa said in a surprisingly nice voice as she beamed at Ben and smoothed down her short cheerleading skirt and matching fitted top.

"Well, I will now that Campbell has helped me out," he assured her before galloping across the courts. Once he had gone, Sophie took a deep breath and started to speak before Melissa could open her mouth.

"Okay, so I know what you're thinking, but I promise that nothing happened. Nothing. I mean, the only reason I let him touch the guitar pick was because he's your boyfriend. I thought that it might make you like me more, and—"

"Relax," Melissa commanded as she held up a perfectly

manicured hand. "I'm not going to bite your head off. I actually just saw that you'd signed up for the tryouts and wanted to say that, if you like, I could help you out a little."

"Y-you can?" Sophie blinked as she realized that Melissa was actually smiling. Did that mean she was being nice two times in under a minute? Surely that had to be some kind of record. Then she narrowed her eyes. "Did Jonathan bribe you to say that?"

"Of course not. For a start, Jonathan is a complete amateur when it comes to bribing anyone," Melissa said, like that was a bad thing. Then, when Sophie didn't look convinced, she let out a sigh. "Okay, so here's the thing. Even though Jonathan and I aren't exactly the 'joined at the hips' kind of twins, he's still my brother, and I figure if he likes you, I should at least make an attempt to get to know you. I mean, we must have something in common."

"That's exactly what I said, when my friends and Jonathan tried to tell me trying out was a bad idea," Sophie exclaimed in excitement. *See, she knew the Universe wouldn't let her down.*

"Well, just shows what they all know." Melissa shot her a conspiratorial wink before frowning. "Of course, it doesn't guarantee you're going to make the squad. You've still got to impress Miss Carson, and there are a few other contenders for Donna's spot."

"I've got a few tricks up my sleeve," Sophie said as she

resisted the urge to grin. *She knew that this had been a good plan.*

"I hope so, because I'm starting to think that this might be fun. Anyway, come on. Miss Carson is waiting, and you still need to get changed."

"Changed?" Sophie blinked as she looked down at her ill-fitting gym shorts and her oversize T-shirt. "Can't I just do the tryouts in this?"

"Rule number one if you want to be friends with me. Always dress the part." Melissa made a clicking noise with her tongue as she nodded for Sophie to follow her. As they headed toward the locker room, Sophie glanced over to Harvey, who just held up his arms and shrugged, as if to agree that Sophie's plan hadn't been such a dumb idea after all.

"Huh, well, I didn't expect that it would fit quite so well," Melissa said in surprise when Sophie stepped out of the changing cubicle. Then she brightened. "I suppose that means it's a sign you should be on the team, right?"

"I hope so." Sophie returned the smile and crossed her fingers, since her well-fitting outfit was actually a result of djinn magic rather than a sign from the Universe. She glanced down at her skirt. While it wasn't quite as fitted as Melissa's was, at least it no longer trailed down below Sophie's knees. And she had managed to make the top, which had obviously been designed for someone with a large chest, a better fit for her almost nonexistent boobs. Unfortunately, there was nothing she could do to make the cat-vomit yellow stop clashing with her pale hair, but at least she no longer looked like a little girl who had just raided her big sister's closet.

"Great, so let's get out there," Melissa said as they hurried back onto the court, where Miss Carson was blowing her whistle.

"Quiet, please, ladies," the coach called out as all the wannabe cheerleaders crowded around her. "Melissa's going to take you through a warm-up, and then we'll start the tryouts. Clear?"

Everyone nodded and formed three lines while Melissa marched to the front. Sophie managed to find a spot as far toward the back as she could and took a deep breath. So far her plan was working, but it really all hung on how good her transcendental wishing skills were. Before she could worry, Melissa clapped her hands and started the warm-ups.

Ten minutes later, despite her panting, Sophie couldn't help but conceal a grin since normally she couldn't manage more than ten lunges in a row, but thanks to her wishing skills, she had done thirty. Even Miss Carson had looked impressed. But real proof was going to be when she did her own routine.

Thankfully, she had managed to get last in line, which meant that she could watch everyone else and study their moves. Finally, it was her turn. She was just about to start when Melissa hurried over to her.

"Hey, I just want to wish you luck." Melissa grinned.

"You do?" Sophie widened her eyes, still not quite able to take in the personality change in Jonathan's twin sister.

"Don't look so surprised," Melissa said as she reached out and smoothed down Sophie's uniform. Then her face wrinkled in concern. "Oh, you forgot to take your watch and jewelry off."

Sophie looked at her blankly. "Was I supposed to?"

"Um, yeah." Melissa nodded her head. "The reason Donna broke her leg was because her foot got caught around a necklace that Amber Smith was wearing, so now it's a new rule. And since Miss Carson came up with the rule, she might take points off if you ignore it."

Sophie quickly started to tug at her watch and her other jewelry and passed them over to Melissa. "Will you hold them for me while I do the tryout?"

"Of course I will." Melissa beamed. "Anything to help you make the team." Then she walked back to the judging table, where she and the other cheerleaders were sitting. Once she was gone Sophie loosened her shoulders and headed to the center of the floor. She took a deep breath before she concentrated on visualizing herself doing the routine. She could do this.

She was a strong and positive person. Not to mention a djinn. She was going to nail this routine. For herself. For Jonathan. And for her dad.

She grinned as a familiar tingle went racing through her and she felt her physical body and the image in her mind merge into one. The music started, and Sophie made her first move. Her body twisted and prepared to turn and then... *she felt herself fall into an undignified heap on the floor.*

Okay, so that definitely wasn't part of the plan. She tried to ignore the laughter that was springing up from all around her. Instead, she focused on getting to her feet and trying to redo the move. However, despite visualizing every step, the second time she attempted the turn she fell to the ground even harder.

"Right, Sophie, well, that was an *interesting* routine." Miss Carson blew her whistle to signal that the tryouts were over. "Thank you to everyone who came out today. We'll be posting the name of the new member outside my office tomorrow."

Without another word Miss Carson headed toward the exit as Harvey came racing over.

"Are you okay? What happened?"

"I've got no idea." Sophie shook her head as she awkwardly got to her feet. "I mean, one minute everything was perfect, and then suddenly it wasn't. I guess I haven't quite mastered the transcendental conjuring stuff after all."

"I knew this was a bad idea," he reminded her before letting out a sigh. "But don't beat yourself up about it. It could've been a lot worse."

"Worse than humiliating myself in front of the entire school?" Sophie raised an eyebrow.

"Well, first of all, it wasn't the entire school, it was

about twenty people; and second, it could've happened in front of the Djinn Council," he pointed out.

"You're right. I can't believe I lost my focus like that." Sophie flushed as she realized she had been so concerned about Jonathan and trying to make Melissa like her that she had forgotten about fine-tuning her skills. "I wonder if we have time to go see Malik before next period? Maybe he can tell me why my routine didn't work."

"If it involves leaving the gym, then I'm all for it," Harvey said as they headed for the exit. Sophie glanced at her watch, only to realize it wasn't there. She let out a groan.

"Oh, man, I forgot to get my stuff from Melissa. I had to take all my jewelry off and give it to her just before I did my routine. I'll be only a second," Sophie said as she hurried back to the table where the cheerleaders had been sitting.

Sophie waited until Melissa closed the folder she had been writing in, and when she looked up, Sophie gave her a little wave. However, instead of returning it, Melissa stared right through her before standing up and heading for the exit.

"Hey, wait up," Sophie puffed as she hurried to catch up with Melissa and her long legs.

"I beg your pardon?" Melissa suddenly stopped and turned around, her brown eyes narrowed and menacing and her tone dripping with icicles. "Are you speaking to me?"

"Er." Sophie paused and blinked for a moment as she

realized that she had been a bit premature to think that Melissa had started to like her. Was this because she had screwed up the tryouts? Then she remembered that she had more important things to worry about. Like learning to nail her magic so she could impress the Djinn Council. "Um, yeah, I wanted to get my jewelry back from you. I gave you two rings, a bracelet, my watch, and, of course, the necklace with my Neanderthal Joe guitar pick on it."

"Sorry, I don't know what you're talking about." Melissa shrugged before she folded her arms tightly in front of her chest.

For a moment Sophie just stared at the other girl as she tried to figure out what was going on. *And what had Harvey told her about arm folding being a declaration of war?* A prickle of alarm went racing through her.

"B-but you do. I gave them to you. Right before I did my routine," Sophie reminded her as she thought how much she loved her guitar pick. Granted, she didn't think it was a good-luck charm like Ben Griggs did, but it still symbolized when she and Jonathan had first had their moment.

"I don't think so." Melissa shot her a blank look as she flicked her perfect blonde hair over one shoulder and started to inspect her fingernails. "Oh, but come to think of it, now that you don't have that stupid guitar pick, you'll no longer have an excuse to hang all over my boyfriend. *Gee, that's too bad.*"

"Is that what this is about?" Sophie widened her eyes

as she started to understand what was going on. "The guitar pick? Because I thought I explained that it wasn't my fault that Ben keeps wanting to touch it. I even tried to talk him out of it before because I didn't want to make you mad."

"Really?" Melissa gave a disinterested sniff. "Well, unfortunately, I don't believe you. Still, now that you no longer have it, I guess it's not a problem."

Sophie stared at her. "But what happened to the whole trying to get along with me because I'm a friend of Jonathan's?"

"Please, you're so gullible." Melissa rolled her eyes. "Now seriously, I need to go, because talking to you is giving me a headache."

"You are unbelievable! If you think for a minute that I'm going to let you keep my guitar pick, then you've got another think coming. Besides, Jonathan told me that you don't even like Neanderthal Joe. Now I want you to give me back all of my stuff right now."

"Um, I don't think so. Even if I did have them—which I don't—what could you possibly do to make me change my mind?"

"Let's just say that you don't want to find out," Sophie retorted as a flash of annoyance went racing through her. Honestly, she was tempted to give Melissa a hooknose and split ends, but as she glanced over to the door, she realized that Harvey was impatiently waiting for her. Fine.

Instead, she looked directly into Melissa's dark eyes. "I *wish* you would give all of my jewelry back to me."

As she spoke a familiar tingle went racing through her. Ha. Suck on that, Melissa Tait, Sophie thought as she held out her hand so she could retrieve her stuff. However, after a moment she realized that Melissa was just staring at her. *Okay, so that was weird.* This time Sophie closed her eyes and concentrated.

"I *really* wish that you would give me my stuff back." Again there was the familiar tingle, but instead of the wish manifesting itself like it normally did, Melissa just narrowed her eyes and glared.

"Okay, since you seem to be particularly stupid today, let me spell it out for you. *Not. Going. To. Happen.* Oh, and FYI, whatever little tricks you've been doing to impress people aren't going to work anymore. Do you understand me?"

Then, without another word, Melissa marched out of the gym. As soon as she was gone, Harvey ran over, and this time Kara was with him.

"Harvey told me what happened. You poor thing." Kara gave her a hug, her pale green eyes full of concern. "I knew I should've come here instead of going to the stupid audition. Anyway, Harvey seemed to think that Melissa looked angry, though I'm pretty sure that she always looks like that. Is everything okay?"

"No, everything's *not* okay." Sophie shook her head in

disbelief. "Melissa Tait won't give me back my stuff. It's because she's annoyed that Ben keeps wanting to touch the guitar pick. But that's no reason to steal it from me. I mean it's Eddie Henry's guitar pick. I can't believe she thinks that she can just keep it."

"So why didn't you just wish for her to give them back?" Harvey pushed his long bangs out of his eyes.

"I did." Sophie tried not to panic. "But for some strange reason it didn't work. I-I think my magic's gone."

10

"WHAT DO YOU MEAN IT'S GONE?" HARVEY BLINKED a few minutes later as they all huddled together in the janitor's closet. "How can it just be gone?"

"I don't know." Sophie shot him a helpless look.

"Okay, so the important thing is not to panic," Harvey said in a panicked voice.

"Look," Kara chimed in, "I'm sure there's a completely logical explanation for all of this. Maybe Malik forgot to tell Sophie that there's a limit on how much magic she could use in one day? I mean, that totally sounds like something he would do."

"Actually, it does," Harvey said, looking a bit less worried.

"None of this is helping me," Sophie pointed out. "Especially since Malik isn't here." She clapped her hands, but there was no sign of the djinn ghost. "Where is he?"

"I don't know," Kara wailed. "He said that if he had to watch one more person murder "We're Off to See the Wizard" at the auditions, he would eat his iPod. Then he got a phone call and went off to take it. I just assumed he had come here."

"Maybe he went to the bathroom?" Harvey suggested.

"He's a ghost. I'm pretty sure that he doesn't need to use the bathroom anymore," Sophie reminded her friend before letting out a groan. "I still don't understand. I made Mr. Pugsy fly, but now I can't even make that mop lift off the ground." They all stared at the mop, but it refused to move. Harvey gave a polite cough.

"Maybe you should try something simple like wishing for a bag of M&M's?" he said.

"Harvey, I don't think—" Kara started to say, but Harvey shook his head.

"No, I didn't mean for a snack, I just meant as an experiment."

"Oh." Kara looked embarrassed. "Actually, that's a good idea."

"I've been trying to wish for things for the last few minutes, but I've got nothing," Sophie said, barely resisting the urge to panic. "Not even a bag of Cheetos—and I swear I've conjured up so many of them that sometimes I make them appear in my sleep."

"Like I said, I'm sure there's a logical explanation for all of this," Kara responded in an unusually firm voice just as the bell rang. "But until you speak to Malik, you're just going to have to stay calm and try not to panic."

Despite Kara's pep talk, the next two classes went by with agonizing slowness, with still no sign of either Malik or her magical powers. By the time the last class was finished, Sophie jumped to her feet, eager to get home to try to figure out just what was going on.

Kara had promised to go to the Art Department and work on Colin the winged monkey, and Harvey was going to view another apartment with his dad after school, so Sophie ended up catching the bus by herself. They had both asked if she wanted them to cancel their plans, but she had refused. Not because she could panic just as easily on her own, but because she had to babysit Meg, and she was sure her friends could do without playing three games of shark.

She ignored the jostling and yelling of the kids around her as the bus made its stop-start journey. Instead, she continued to try to figure out what was going on. *Maybe Kara was right and Malik had forgotten to warn her about using too much power in one day? Or could it be some kind of test that the Djinn Council was giving her?* Actually, that kind of made sense, Sophie decided, as the bus pulled up to her stop and she got off. Not that she really understood what they could achieve by testing her on how she coped without her powers, but then again, according to Malik, the Djinn Council wasn't exactly logical.

"So how did it go?" Her mom immediately wanted to know as Sophie walked into the kitchen. "Are you going to be the next Paula Abdul?"

"Not quite." Sophie shook her head as she tried not to notice the large collection of toilet paper rolls with shark faces drawn on them that were sitting on the kitch-en table. Meg had obviously been raiding the recycling closet in her classroom. "Let's just say it didn't quite go as planned."

"Ah. I think I know what this is about."

"You do?" Sophie, who had just bitten into one of the Oreos that her mom had passed to her, looked at her in surprise.

"I do." Her mom nodded. "You're worried that Jona-than saw you trying out and that now he will think less of you."

Sophie felt an Oreo crumb lodge in her throat as she stared at her mom. She had been too busy worrying about the fact that Melissa had taken her guitar pick and that she'd lost her powers; she hadn't stopped to consider if Jonathan had seen her embarrassing performance.

"But trust me," her mom continued. "If you two are meant to be friends, then nothing will stop that."

"I hope you're right." Sophie sighed as she idly fiddled with a piece of paper that was sitting on the table. Then she wrinkled her nose as she studied it more carefully. It looked like some kind of building quote. "What's this?"

"Oh." Her mom winced as she plucked the piece of paper out of Sophie's hands. "That's how much it's going to cost to get the studio leak repaired. I knew it would be bad, but I wasn't expecting it to be that bad."

"What?" Sophie spluttered, since there were a lot of

zeroes in the figure. Especially considering that she could fix the leak with a wish. *Well, when she had her magic, she could.* She looked at her mom in concern; normally it was a big deal if they got Chinese takeout, let alone made a big repair like that. "What are you going to do?"

"Not much right now." Her mom shook her head. "I can't afford the repairs, so I'm going to have to move my whole studio down into the basement. It's just such bad timing."

"I guess that makes sense, though won't it be a bit cramped?" Sophie wondered, since despite all the stuff she had magically moved yesterday, there was still plenty more down there. Then she noticed that her mom was busy studying the quote. "What's going on?"

"I was thinking of sorting through your father's boxes and donating some of his things to the thrift store," her mom said, still not looking up.

"What?" Sophie felt her throat tighten, and her heart began to pound in her chest as she realized that Meg had been totally right yesterday.

"I'm sorry. I know this is going to be hard on you."

"Which is why you shouldn't do it," Sophie told her. "Besides, there're plenty of other things down there that could go. Meg doesn't need her tricycle anymore, and you can definitely get rid of my old *Girl2day* magazines. I mean, I had planned to keep them in case I ever wanted to use them for a project, but this isn't about me. It's about you, and if it will make you happy, then I'll get rid of them. Besides, you told me the other day that you don't hate him anymore."

"And I meant it. I will always love your father, but the last couple of weeks have been a real eye-opener for me, and getting back into my pottery has really helped. I don't need to sell the house to move on, but I think it's time that I make some other changes. Ones that will help us get financially secure again. Remember what I said yesterday? That the things down there don't hold memories. The memories are in our mind."

"Yes, but Dad *isn't* a memory. He's coming back, and when he does, he'll need his things. Please," Sophie begged. She longed to tell her mom how close she was to finding out the truth about him, but she knew she couldn't. At least not until she had some proof. Not to mention that she would have to explain the whole "Hey, Mom. Guess what? I'm actually a djinn" thing first.

"I wish it was that simple. Perhaps when you're older you will understand that sometimes things are complicated."

"Mom, I *do* understand how complicated things sometimes are," Sophie assured her as she tried not to think about today's disaster. *Boy, did she understand complicated.* "But you have to believe me that throwing away Dad's things would be a bad idea."

"Sophie, I know you believe he's coming back, but after

four years of waiting, I've finally realized that I can't stay in limbo anymore. And until I can afford to get the studio fixed, I need to make room down there. I was thinking that tomorrow you and Meg could help me. We can all do it together."

"Tomorrow?" Sophie stared at her in alarm. "That's too soon. I've got loads of things to do. Er, like homework." *And getting her magic back so she could fix the leak and save her dad's boxes from going to the thrift store.* "You've got to wait a bit longer. How about another year? Or at least another month? A lot can happen between now and then."

"Or, nothing could change," her mom countered before letting out a reluctant sigh. "Fine, I'll hold off until Saturday. But Sophie, until my studio is fixed I'm going to need to use the basement, and all the positive thinking in the world can't change that. Anyway, this probably isn't the best time to discuss it since I'm supposed to be meeting Max."

At that moment Meg wandered in, spotted the Oreos, and immediately crammed one into her mouth. Sophie didn't have the heart to tell her she had been right about what their mom was planning. Besides, as soon as Sophie got her magic back, the whole problem would be easily solved.

"That's enough," her mom said, as Meg attempted to shove two more Oreos into her mouth at the same time. She was putting the rest of the cookies back into the packet just as Mr. Jaws poked his head in to see what was going on. "And now I really do need to go."

"Hey," Meg suddenly said as she scooped the cat into an undignified bundle and held him up in the air. "He isn't hissing at Sophie anymore. He must like her again."

"Gee, lucky old me," Sophie retorted, while secretly realizing her sister was right. For the first time in ages Mr. Jaws hardly even seemed to notice she was there. Obviously all the cat-snack bribing she had been doing for the last three and a half weeks was finally paying off.

"Mr. Jaws has always liked Sophie," their mom quickly said in an unconvincing voice, but before Meg could do more than make a snorting noise, their mom grabbed her car keys and gave them both a kiss good-bye.

The moment their mom was gone Meg glared at her. "I told you so."

"Told me what?" Sophie started to say before realizing that Meg had been listening in on the conversation. She gave her a stern frown. "You need to stop doing that. And besides, you don't need to worry, because by Saturday the studio will be all better and Mom won't need to move into the basement."

"How is that possible?" Meg demanded, her shrewd eyes studying Sophie's face intently.

"Don't you worry about that," Sophie said vaguely since she could hardly tell her the truth. "But just trust me that nothing is going to happen to Dad's boxes. I promise."

"Humph," Meg said in a noncommittal voice before she tugged at Sophie's sleeve and dragged her into the back garden. Sophie let out a groan as she let herself be pulled along. The afternoon sunshine was still coming through the clouds in patches, while Mr. Jaws energetically chased a fly around the overgrown grass. The large sheet of black plastic that was covering the corner of their mom's pottery studio made a light flapping noise as the wind caught it. Sophie paused for a moment and glared at it. Stupid leak.

Over on the other side of the fence, Jessica Dalton was halfheartedly playing with a plastic toy, but the minute she saw Meg, she shot her a hopeful smile. Meg ignored her completely and instead turned to Sophie.

"So now it's time to play shark," her sister announced. "I have decided that you will be a shrimp and I'm going to be a great white, and you have to try to escape from me or taste my terrible wrath."

"I'm a one-inch shrimp and you're a ginormous great white?" Sophie raised an eyebrow, momentarily distracted. "How is that fair?"

"There's nothing fair about nature, Sophie," Meg reminded her in an earnest voice before shaking her blonde ringlets. "Besides, great whites are awesome, and it's my game, which means I get to choose what I want to be."

"Fine—" Sophie started to say before she glanced up to her bedroom window and realized Malik was standing there looking like he didn't have a care in the world. As soon as he saw her looking at him, he gave her a hearty wave. About time. Sophie turned back to her sister. "Er, Meggy, would you mind if I just go up to my room for a while?"

"Yes, I mind," Meg replied in a blunt voice. "You promised to play three games of shark with me, and now it's time for you to taste my terrible wrath."

"I know, but this is important," Sophie insisted. She felt bad trying to fob her sister off, especially in light of the whole basement thing. But then again, the sooner she spoke to Malik, the sooner she would get her powers back and the pottery shed crisis could be solved. Sophie glanced around, looking for inspiration. Her sight settled on Jessica, who was still peering over the fence with interest. "Why don't you get Jessica to play sharks with you and taste your terrible wrath?"

"Because she hates sharks," Meg retorted, still refusing to look over the fence.

"I'm sure that she doesn't really hate sharks," Sophie said in a cajoling voice, determined to get the two girls talking again. Then she turned to Jessica. "Do you?"

"No, I don't," Jessica chimed in. "I like sharks."

"Since when?" Meg demanded, her back still turned.

"Since my mom bought me a book on them. Bull sharks are my favorite," Jessica replied, and Meg reluctantly turned around an inch.

"Bull sharks are pretty cool," she conceded before narrowing her eyes. "But do you think a bull shark could beat a dinosaur in a fight?"

"Totally." Jessica was now leaning over the fence, an excited glint in her eyes. "In the book my mom got me it said that bull sharks can live in salt water and freshwater. You don't see any dinosaurs living in two kinds of air, do you?"

"Exactly," Meg responded with a knowing nod. "Not to mention dinosaurs were dumb enough to get themselves extinct. So what other kinds of sharks do you like?"

"All sorts," Jessica said as she held up a plastic shark; Meg instantly grabbed it and started inspecting its teeth to see how sharp they were. Then, when she nodded her head in approval, Jessica shot her a hopeful glance and said, "Hey, do you want to come over and see the shark-shaped cookies that my mom made for me? She made some for you, too. Just in case …"

Meg didn't even blink as she jumped over the fence and followed Jessica into her house without so much as a backward glance. At her kitchen window Mrs. Dalton waved over to Sophie to let her know that she would take care of the girls.

Sophie let out a sigh of relief. Now that Meg was happy she could talk to Malik. As she hurried up to her room, she crossed her fingers that the rest of her problems could be so easily solved.

11

"WHERE HAVE YOU BEEN?" SOPHIE DEMANDED THE minute she burst into her bedroom, where Malik was standing by the window smiling serenely. "I've been clapping for you all afternoon."

"Um, I don't think so." Malik shook his head. He wandered over to the computer table and sat down on the swivel chair. "Because if you had clapped me, I would've appeared. That's what helpful djinns do."

"Oh, really?" Sophie queried as she raised an eyebrow. "So what about all the other times I clapped you and you never bothered to turn up?"

"That's different," Malik explained, looking completely unrepentant. "Because then I knew you were clapping me, but I just chose to ignore it—not that that's very easy, since you can be quite persistent when you put your mind to it. But the point is that you most definitely didn't summon me today."

Sophie opened her mouth before shutting it again. Getting distracted in a Malik argument wasn't really on her agenda right now. "Okay, summoning aside, I really need to talk to you. Something weird happened at the tryouts today."

"It did? What? *Oh, don't you tell me that Zac Efron turned up.* I should never have let Kara talk me into going to those stupid auditions." Malik looked mutinous, but Sophie quickly shook her head.

"No, Zac Efron, the international movie star, did *not* turn up to the Robert Robertson Middle School cheerleading tryouts. Now can you please try to focus, because this is important. Halfway through the tryouts, I suddenly lost all of my power, and…why are you laughing?"

"Sorry." Malik put his hand over his mouth to try to hide the fact he was grinning from ear to ear. "It's just that you're acting so serious about nothing."

"You think that losing my power is nothing?" Sophie blinked at him.

"No, that's not what I'm saying. The thing is that it's impossible for a djinn to lose her power. It just doesn't happen. Hence my mirth."

"Well, it's happened to me," Sophie insisted. "So now we need to figure out why. Kara thought that maybe you forgot to tell me about a quota on how much power you can use on one day?"

"Do I look like I would forget to tell you something

like that?" Malik gave an offended sniff before shaking his head. "And besides, there's nothing to forget. There's no limit on how much power you can access."

Huh, well, that wasn't the answer that she'd been hoping to hear . She licked her lips and shot him a hopeful glance. "So is it possible that the Djinn Council is putting me through some kind of top-secret test?"

"Trust me, that bunch of old women couldn't keep a secret if their immortal lives depended on it. Blabber mouths, every single one of them. When they test you, you will know about it." Malik shuddered before realizing she was still waiting for him to answer her. "Anyway, like I said, it's impossible to lose your powers. I mean, as long as you still have your djinn ring, then your powers are yours to control and... *Okay, so why isn't your djinn ring on your finger?*"

"What?" Sophie blinked as she glanced down and looked at her finger. Her finger that was completely free of her gorgeous apple-shaped, rhinestone-studded ring. She let out a long groan. "As well as my watch and my Neanderthal Joe guitar pick, Melissa Tait still has my ring. You know, she is so unbelievable, and I tried to get it all back after the tryouts, but she refused—" Sophie suddenly paused as she realized Malik was looking at her in horror. "Oh, has that got something to do with the fact I've lost my powers?"

"Um, yeah." He continued to stare at her in disbelief.

"Are you seriously telling me that you gave someone else your djinn ring? Of your own free will?"

Sophie reluctantly nodded as she realized she had been so distracted with Melissa Tait taking her Neanderthal Joe guitar pick that she hadn't give her djinn ring a second thought. She was now guessing that this had been a mistake.

"Are you insane?" Malik had now stood up and was pacing the room in a very agitated manner, before he finally came to a halt and turned to her. "What is the first rule of being a djinn?"

"Never wish for anything bigger than your head when you are in a confined space?" Sophie joked, while trying not to be thrown by the uncharacteristically grim expression on his face.

"No." Malik didn't look remotely amused. "That's rule number fifty-three. Rule number one is never to give away your djinn ring. To anyone. *Ever.* I think you'd better write it down."

Sophie chewed her lip. Now that he mentioned it, it did sound vaguely familiar, but when he had first told her, it hadn't really mattered because when she did try to take the ring off, she was hit with waves of unrelenting pain. And then when she had finally finished cleansing the ring, she hadn't bothered to take it off much because it looked so good with everything. She took a deep breath and reminded herself that she was a positive person.

djinns a bit better. Not that it worked, since that dude was one lousy boss."

"I see," Sophie gulped as she studied Malik's face. "So the elixir's out, too. Tell me, is there any chance that the third way of breaking a bind is actually something I might stand a chance of being able to do?"

"Let's hope so." Malik's voice suddenly sounded softer and full of concern. "Because the third way of breaking a bind is to convince the sahir in question to return your djinn ring of her own free will."

"That's it?" Sophie blinked at him since she had been expecting something more along the lines of goat fur and a full moon with maybe a sprinkle of eye of newt thrown in for good measure. In fact, if she still had her powers, she would probably wish away all of Malik's *High School Musical* paraphernalia just to teach him not to scare her like that. "That's all I have to do to get out of this thing? Because I can fix that right now. I'll just call Jonathan and explain what's happened—apart from all the crazy djinn business, of course—then he can use whatever dirt he has on his sister to make her give me the djinn ring back. Simple."

"Yeah, so let me give you a crash course in how free will works." Malik shook his head. "It can't be done with coercion. The sahir has to want to give it back to you. In fact, the free-will option never normally works on sahirs because they are such evil and cunning creatures with a single-minded determination to make our lives miserable."

"But you're forgetting that while Melissa is definitely evil and cunning, she has no idea what my ring means," Sophie reminded him in a positive voice. "Honestly, Malik, I can't understand why you're being so negative. I'll get my ring back tomorrow, and everything will be fine. I mean, I managed to live the last eleven years without magic, so I think I can last a day or so. And when I do get it back, I'll even conjure you up some extra Cheetos to celebrate. Okay?"

However, before Malik could answer there was a flapping noise and a pink pigeon suddenly appeared in the room, with a letter in its beak. The minute it saw Malik, the bird rustled its feathers in annoyance, causing all of Sophie's homework to go flying around the room. Then it dropped the letter onto the ground and disappeared, not even bothering to wait for a tip. But Sophie hardly noticed as she recognized the Djinn Council logo on the top of the letter. She snatched it up and tried to ignore the way her hands shook as she opened it.

Dear Initiate,

After careful consideration we have decided to agree to your request to change your appointment time. You are now required to meet with us on the fifth hand of the Rosewood eclipse, where you will undergo a standard Phoenician test before you can proceed with your aforementioned interview. Please do not re-spond directly to this letter as it will not be read. Also, you shall note that the Djinn Council does not take kindly to tar-diness, so arrive on time or not at all.

    Yours,

    Leshanka the Odious

    Djinn Council General Undersecretary and Translator

Sophie turned to Malik and waved the letter. "You did it. You got them to change the interview time. This is perfect. All I need to do now is get my ring back and start practicing," she exclaimed before noticing that Malik was still very subdued. "What's wrong? Are you going to tell me that the Rosewood eclipse is even further away than my original appointment?"

"No, unfortunately, it's not further away," Malik said, his tone unusually somber. "In fact, it's this week."

"W-what?" Sophie felt her good mood plummet. "Are you sure?"

Malik nodded. "According to this, your appointment to see the Djinn Council is now this Saturday at ten o'clock."

"What? But tomorrow's Thursday, which means that I have only two days to prepare?" Sophie's good mood immediately disappeared as she realized that trying to do a transcendental conjuring trick without her djinn ring might be a bit complicated. She took a deep breath and turned to Malik. "W-what are their thoughts on talking to djinns who have been bound?"

"I hate to be the one to tell you, but if you're bound, they won't even let you through the door. And they weren't joking about not liking tardiness. I remember this one time that Rene—"

But Sophie hardly heard. Instead, she concentrated on chanting a positive affirmation over and over again. *I am a strong and positive person, and I will get my djinn ring back by ten o'clock Saturday. Because the alternative isn't worth thinking about....*

12

ANY LUCK?" HARVEY DEMANDED THE MINUTE
Sophie arrived at her locker the following morning.

"No." Sophie shook her head. She had been searching for Melissa for the last twenty minutes with no success whatsoever. Which was ironic, really, since lately it
seemed like wherever Sophie turned around, Melissa was
standing there, looking down her nose. Of course, if she'd
had her magic, she would've asked Malik to teach her how
to do a locator wish, but unfortunately, she couldn't do
that until *after* she got her ring back.

And not that she would admit it to Malik, but she was
surprised at how much she already missed having her
djinn powers. Not least when her mom had handed her a
plate of scrambled eggs for breakfast and they had been a
gray color instead of yellow and white. Normally, Sophie
would've wished for them to taste like chocolate crois-
sants, but instead she had been forced to eat them as they

were, unlike her sister, who had scampered over to Jessica Dalton's for pancakes and maple syrup.

Unfortunately, the bad breakfast hadn't taken her mind off the fact that she had managed to get herself bound two days before she was due to perform in front of the Djinn Council in order to ask them to help her find her father. Talk about bad timing.

"Are you sure you can't just change your appointment?" Kara asked, somehow knowing that Sophie had been thinking about it. She reluctantly shook her head, since she had asked Malik that very same question (more than once).

"Apparently, even changing it once is a really big request, and there's no way they will consider doing it again. But that's okay," Sophie quickly assured her friends in a bright voice, "because as long as I get my ring back from Melissa today, then I'll still have tonight and tomorrow to practice. I'm sure it will be plenty of time."

"Of course it will," Kara immediately agreed in a supportive voice. "So have you figured out what you're going to say to her when you do find her?"

"Yes, I'm going to appeal to her better nature."

"I hate to be negative, but I don't think she has one of those," the normally kindhearted Kara said.

"I know it's a long shot, but as a positive person I have to give her the benefit of the doubt. However, if she still refuses, then I will simply go and see Miss Carson. I mean, she was at the tryouts yesterday and saw what happened. *And* she knows that the ring is mine: remember she was trying to make me take it off when we played basketball the other day?"

"Those are both nice practical solutions." Harvey coughed as he walked along next to them, his long legs easily matching Sophie's jog. "But I think you will find that I have a completely foolproof plan. All you need to do is tell her that the ring is a family heirloom, and that if anyone who isn't in your direct bloodline wears it, then that person will be cursed for all eternity. And by cursed I mean covered with boils." He grinned as he nodded his head in excitement. "Nice, right?"

Sophie blinked. "You want me to tell her the ring is cursed?"

"What's wrong with that?" Harvey protested. "You see that kind of stuff in horror movies all the time. *Oh, you should mention that the curse includes pus as well. No one wants to get cursed with pus-filled boils.*"

"It sounds stupid to me," Malik suddenly announced in a grim voice from up by the ceiling.

"What's his problem?" Kara wrinkled her nose.

"Just ignore him," Sophie advised. "He's been in a bad mood ever since he found out I gave my ring to Melissa. I think he feels guilty, which is stupid, because I'm going to get it back today and everything will be fine." Then she looked up to where Malik was still hovering. "Are you sure you don't want to go and wait in the janitor's closet for me?"

"What? So you can screw up even more? I don't think so."

"Malik, I'm not going to make another mistake," Sophie informed him, but before he could answer, Melissa and her Tait-bots suddenly appeared at the other end of the hallway. Speak of the devil. Sophie gulped as she realized this was her chance, and so she hurried over.

"Oh, it's you. I hope you're not bothering to see if you made the squad," Melissa said in a frosty voice.

"No," Sophie assured her. "All I want is to get my stuff that you were holding yesterday afternoon back."

"Well, that's too bad because I threw it out."

"You what?" Sophie yelped as she felt a sliver of panic go racing through her. "How could you throw it out?"

"Because that stupid guitar pick didn't work. I mean, ever since you got it, Ben's been all over you like a wet rag. But when I tried it, he said it felt funny, and then he failed his Spanish quiz, which means that he's going to be benched for today's game. *A whole game.* And get this. He thinks it's my fault."

"It is your fault. You stole my stuff. And I can't believe you threw out the guitar pick that Eddie Henry gave me." Sophie quivered in annoyance, not quite able to comprehend what Melissa had just told her. Not only had the pick come from the greatest bass player in the entire world, she had also gotten it on the same night that she and Jonathan had shared their moment. In other words, it was so much more than just a guitar pick.

Then she suddenly realized that there was one thing worse than Melissa's throwing the pick away. An uneasy prickle went up the back of her neck.

"W-what about my other stuff? There was a ring. It was apple-shaped with rhinestones on it. Please tell me that you didn't throw that out, too?"

"What?" Melissa blinked before she gave a casual wave of her hand. "Oh, right. That thing. No, though seriously, I would be doing you a favor if I did. Ugly much?"

"Excuse me, but my ring is not ugly," Sophie said in a tight voice as she tried to stay calm. All she needed to do was appeal to Melissa's better nature and get her ring back, then she could dislike her as much as she wanted. "And the point is that I really, really need to get it back."

"Yes, well, I need to get my boyfriend back, but thanks to that stupid guitar pick of yours, it doesn't look like that's going to happen."

"Melissa, I'm serious. That ring's really important." Sophie earnestly nodded her head, because Harvey had once told her that it was a classic body-language trick to get someone to agree with you. Or was that the Jedi mind trick? Anyway, all Sophie knew was that she would try anything that might help her right now.

"And my boyfriend isn't?"

So much for better nature. Sophie felt the blood start

to pound around her temples as she realized just how serious this situation was. If she didn't get her ring back, then she would be stuck taking orders from Melissa Tait forever. And it was bad enough talking to her for five minutes.

Sophie licked her lips. "Okay, so I'm willing to overlook the guitar pick and the watch, but I really need my ring back, and if you won't give it to me, I'll have to go see Miss Carson about it."

"No, you won't."

"Yes, I will," Sophie insisted. "In fact, I'm going to go to her office right now and—"

"Excuse me, but you're not going anywhere," Melissa corrected in much the same "alpha-queen-of-the-world" voice she used when she was talking to her Tait-bots. "And furthermore, you're not going to say one word about this to any teacher. Do you understand?"

Yeah, right, Sophie started to say as she turned to head in the direction of Miss Carson's office, but instead of moving, her feet stayed exactly where they were. She tried again to lift her foot, this time in the direction of Principal Gerrard's office, but once again, she was stuck to the spot like a statue. She felt the sweat bead on her upper lip as an air of desperation started to surround her.

"O-okay." She tried to hide her mounting panic as she realized that desperate times called for desperate measures. "So what if I tell you that the ring is a family heirloom, and if anyone outside the family wears it, that person will be cursed? Forever. W-with pus and boils."

"Lucky I keep a beautician on retainer then. Anyway, what's the point of worrying about that when Ben thinks that I'm a jinx?" Melissa demanded, her face puckering in annoyance. "I can't believe how selfish you are."

Sophie took a deep breath and tried to stay calm. "Look, I'm sorry if you think I'm being selfish, but if you could just give me the ring back, then—"

"Ring, ring, ring." Melissa rolled her eyes. "You know what? You're like a broken CD the way you go on. Why don't you start singing a new song, because this one is getting boring," she said, before spinning around on her ridiculously high heels and marching away in the other direction.

"Yes, well, that's just—" Sophie started to say before she suddenly felt an overwhelming desire to . . . *sing a song?*

Oh, no. She widened her eyes as she tried to resist, but the minute she did so, she got a stabbing sensation in her stomach that started to spread out around her body. Sophie doubled over in pain, while at the same time shoving her hand over her mouth to stop words from coming out. Okay, so she had no idea what was going on, but she was fairly sure that it wasn't good news. Especially since it made her earlier inability to walk now seem like child's play.

"It's a command, you idiot. The more you try to resist it, the more it's going to hurt," a low voice said in her ear, and she managed to glance up to see Malik hovering beside her, looking pale.

"That's not fair," Kara protested.

"Hello." Malik waved his arms and looked perplexed. "What do you think I've been trying to tell you all? Being bound by a sahir isn't like a visit to a bunny farm, where you just hand in your powers for a couple of days and go off and cuddle some little rabbits. You are completely under her control, and if she tells you to go and jump off a roof, then you will be asking which one," Malik concluded as Kara and Harvey's faces simultaneously drained of color.

"So if Melissa says that Sophie has to sing, then she has to sing?" Harvey demanded, as he looked around at all the people who were milling around their lockers.

"Just do what she asked you to do, and then you will feel better," Malik said, and Sophie let out a small groan before she finally opened her mouth and started to sing her favorite Neanderthal Joe song at the top of her very off-key voice.

This was obviously going to be tougher than Sophie thought.

13

"ARE YOU SURE MELISSA'S EVEN ALLOWED TO DO that?" Harvey demanded as they quickly made their way to class. Sophie tried to avoid noticing the way kids were looking at her (while almost wishing that this really was a scene from *High School Musical*, just so her impromptu singing session wouldn't have been quite so out of place). "I mean, shouldn't there be some kind of sahir code of ethics or something?"

"Like I keep telling you, Sophie's bound to Melissa, which means she's completely under her control," Malik reminded them. "In fact, the only good thing about this whole situation—"

"There's something good about this?" Sophie cut in, her voice a little squeaky. "Did you not just hear me sing? I was like one of those *American Idol* rejects you like to watch on YouTube. It was terrible."

"Well, yes, it is true that you can't hold a tune," Malik

agreed. "But what I meant was that at least Melissa doesn't realize the power she has over you, so she has no idea that you will literally do everything she tells you to do."

"She might not realize that I'm a djinn, but I'm pretty sure that she knows I'm a freak," Sophie muttered as they made their way to the back of their Spanish class and got out their books. "So what do I do now?"

"Obviously, you need to get the ring back from her before she makes you do anything else embarrassing," Harvey said before he wrinkled his nose. "Are you sure you mentioned the pus and boils? Because that should've been a very powerful deterrent."

"Turns out that Melissa laughs in the face of family curses." Sophie sighed as she tried to shake off just how humiliating the whole singing thing had been.

"I think it's pretty obvious what you have to do," Kara said. "I mean, she threw away your Eddie Henry guitar pick and is now refusing to give your ring back. You've got to go with Plan B and tell a teacher. And yes, I know that it's not cool to get your boyfriend's twin sister in trouble, but—"

"I can't." Sophie shook her head. "I stupidly told her that's what I was going to do, and she commanded me not to say a word to any teachers about what had happened."

"Are you sure she commanded you?" Malik puckered his brow, and Sophie nodded her head.

"I think so. I mean, there were no stabbing pains or

anything, but I couldn't move my feet. At all. It was like I had concrete sneakers on."

"Yup," Malik agreed. "That's a command all right. You know, for a novice who doesn't even realize she's a sahir, you've got to admit that Melissa's got a natural flair for it."

They all turned and stared at him, but before Sophie could comment, Señor Rena walked into the room and told everyone to start work on their plurals. Sophie vaguely listened to what he was saying, but for the most part she was too busy trying to figure out a way to get her ring back. Especially since she could not afford another singing episode in the middle of the hallway. The only good news in the whole humiliating debacle was that Jonathan hadn't been around to witness it.

Then she sat up straight as she realized she had the perfect solution. Jonathan. Why hadn't she thought of him sooner? He had specifically invited her to watch him play today (hence why she was wearing her favorite jeans and a cute gray blouse). Not that her outfit really mattered; the point was that Jonathan could help her. Even though Malik had said yesterday that Melissa had to give the ring back of her own free will, the more Sophie thought about it, the more convinced she was that somehow Jonathan could persuade his sister to do the right thing.

Plus, Melissa had only commanded her not to speak to teachers about it. There had been no mention at all of Jonathan, which meant she was free to tell him everything that his evil twin sister had been up to. Including the fact that she had thrown away Eddie Henry's guitar pick. She knew Jonathan would appreciate the offense in that.

Sophie was so lost in thought as she visualized Jonathan's horrified expression that she hardly noticed the bell had rung. It wasn't until Harvey nudged her that she finally got to her feet. A goofy expression lingered on her face as she filled her friends in on the new plan.

"Do you really think this will work?" Kara asked, while next to them Harvey and Malik were bickering over who should get the last M&M. "I mean, I know they're twins, but how can he make her do something she doesn't want to do? And how are you going to ask him without telling him the truth?"

"I don't know, but I'll have to figure it out, because there's no way I can let Melissa boss me around anymore," Sophie said in a firm voice as they made their way to the gymnasium along with half the school. Her eyes scanned the area, finally locating Jonathan at the far end of the court.

As usual he looked all sorts of gorgeous, even despite the fact that Robert Robertson Middle School sport colors were cat-vomit yellow and old-person lilac. As soon as he saw her he gave her a wave, and Sophie felt the tension in her heart ease up as she returned his smile. After the match she would talk to Jonathan, and he would help her get the ring back. Perhaps he would even touch her hand again?

Then she realized that Malik was looking at her oddly, and she felt her face flush. Could djinn ghosts read minds? She certainly hoped not.

"Now I know why we never normally come to these things," Harvey complained as he tried to squeeze past everyone to try to find seats. "Because this crowd is crazy."

"And the other reason we don't come is because we don't like basketball," Kara reminded him.

"How can you not like basketball?" Malik demanded as he floated along next to them. "I mean, it's so athletic, yet skillful. And of course, the dance routines are always catchy.... What? Why are you all looking at me like that?"

"No reason." Harvey looked like he was manfully resisting the urge to laugh. "Though I think you might find that this game is slightly different." Then he leaned forward and widened his eyes. "Hey, Soph, I think that Jonathan is waving for you to go down and see him on the court."

"Really?" Sophie jumped to her feet and started to wish her hair would be less flat before suddenly remembering that she had no magic. Instead, she had to content herself with fluffing it manually before she hurried down to where Jonathan was standing. As she went, Malik gave her one final warning not to let Melissa command her to do any more singing. Well, that was a given.

"Hey." Jonathan shot her an adorable grin. "I'm glad you came."

"Of course I came," Sophie said, before another player suddenly appeared and dragged Jonathan over to where the whole team was in a huddle in the middle of the court. Jonathan gave a rueful shrug. Sophie was just about to turn back to join her friends in the bleachers when Ben Griggs and his giant shoulders suddenly blocked her path.

Unlike Jonathan, he wasn't wearing his basketball gear, and now that she noticed it, he wasn't smiling either. "Campbell, you should never have given the guitar pick to Melissa. She's totally screwed up its mojo, and it doesn't work anymore. I mean, I failed my Spanish quiz, and now I can't play for the rest of the term unless I pass the make-up quiz tomorrow. Maybe that Neanderthal Joe dude gave you something else I could touch?"

"Look, Ben, this isn't a good time," Sophie said. Not just because the game was about to start and she wanted to watch Jonathan play, but because if Melissa saw them talking, she would no doubt blow a fuse. Which was bad enough when she was just plain mean, but now that she actually had control over Sophie as well, it would be disastrous. However, before she could get rid of him she caught sight of Melissa bearing down on them. She was dressed in her cheerleading uniform, and even her pom-poms looked angry. Sophie gulped.

"Oh, what have we here? It's our very own Mariah Carey," Melissa said, her syrupy voice at odds with the hard expression on her face. "So are you going to sing for us again? Or maybe you will dance this time? Because

I'm thinking it would be pretty funny if—"

"Actually," Sophie quickly cut her off, remembering Malik's warning not to let Melissa give her any commands (especially any that involved a potentially embarrassing situation in front of the entire school). "I was just telling Ben how nice your hair looked today."

"Really?" Melissa paused for a moment and shot Ben a hopeful smile. Unfortunately, he totally ignored her. Sophie was guessing that this wasn't a good sign.

"I've got to go," Ben muttered. "Since someone screwed up Sophie's good-luck charm, now if I ever want to play basketball again, I'm going to need to find some moron to explain what my Spanish quiz is all about. I'll know who to blame if I fail it for a second time."

"See." Melissa waited until Ben had stalked off before concentrating her icy glaze back on Sophie again. "He totally thinks this is my fault. You've jinxed me."

"I'm sorry, but you can't blame me for what a guitar pick does or doesn't do," Sophie protested as she wiped her brow and tried to figure out how things had managed to get so complicated. "Now can we please just talk about my ring? I really need it back."

"You know, the more I think about it, the more I'm starting to realize there must be something special about this ring," Melissa suddenly said as she put her hand into her pocket and pulled out a familiar-looking apple-shaped rhinestone-encrusted ring. Sophie widened her eyes. Her ring. Part of her longed simply to reach out and grab it, but then she remembered Malik's words about free will. *Whoever had invented that stupid rule obviously hadn't met Melissa Tait.*

"O-of course there isn't. I just like it," Sophie stammered. Then she looked up and realized that Jonathan was grinning at her from across the court. He did a goofy twirl of the ball, which made Sophie giggle. Melissa immediately stiffened, as too late Sophie realized her mistake.

"Please, don't let me stop you from pulling stupid faces at my brother," the cheerleader snapped in a tight voice, just as Principal Gerrard started to address everyone over the loudspeaker system.

"I wasn't—" Sophie started to reply, but before Sophie knew what was happening, she poked her tongue out at Jonathan Tait and then made her eyes cross. *Nooooooooooooo.* She tried to put her hands across her face to stop it from happening, but instead of covering her face, she found herself putting her hands on each side of her mouth and then wriggling her fingers like there was no tomorrow. Even Meg wouldn't do something so juvenile.

For a moment Jonathan just stared at her in confusion; thankfully, someone suddenly threw a basketball at him, and he turned around to make a shot. Sophie let out a mortified groan while Melissa stared at her in disbelief.

"You are either very stupid or very smart, but either

way I don't really care, as long as you sort out this mess."

"W-what do you mean?" Sophie asked, sure that her cheeks were burning with embarrassment.

"I mean that since it's your fault Ben's mad at me, you can fix it or you can wave good-bye to your precious ring. Oh, and don't try to go blubbing to my brother either. In fact, I don't even want you to look at him again until you've fixed things with Ben and me. Are we clear?"

"No, you don't understand—" Sophie started to say, while trying to ignore the irony that if Melissa would just give her the ring back, she could actually sort the problem out right away. However, before she could say anything else, Melissa suddenly walked away and joined the cheerleaders as Principal Gerrard's speech finally came to an end.

Sophie raced back to where her friends were and sank down into her seat. It was obvious they had figured out what was going on.

"Soph," Harvey started to say, but she shook her head.

"Don't," she begged. "Please, it was too awful for words. She commanded me to make stupid faces at Jonathan. And so I did. It was honestly beyond my control. And it gets worse," she wailed as she filled her friends in on everything that happened.

"See, the girl really is a natural," Malik announced once she had finished. "Notice how she managed to command you to find the solution, while also restricting your chances of actually succeeding in the task itself. It's a classic sahir response. Truly, it's uncanny how skilled she is."

"It's not uncanny, it's evil," Harvey corrected. "I mean, it's not Sophie's fault that Ben sucks at Spanish. It's so unreasonable."

"Er, you do remember this is Melissa Tait that we're talking about," Kara said. "I think she specializes in unreasonable behavior."

"I know." Sophie gave her shoulders and neck a shake to try to get rid of her negative vibes. She turned back to Malik. "Are you sure there isn't another way to get Melissa to give me the ring back? What about that elixir thing you mentioned?"

"You mean the elixir that all djinns have been searching for since the dawn of time?" Malik remarked drily before shaking his head. "Yeah, I think we can safely assume that we won't be finding it before ten o'clock on Saturday."

Sophie felt the desperation rise up and clog in her throat. "Okay, so what about Rufus's Bazaar? He sells everything that a djinn could want through his Web site. Do you think he would have anything that would give me my powers back, even temporarily? Or maybe a mind-control drug so that I can convince Melissa to give me the ring back?"

Again Malik shook his head. "Unfortunately, the Djinn Council banned mind-altering spells about a thousand years ago. It was a very sad day. As for temporary power boosters, I'm afraid that there's no such thing. Oh, but you know what might work? A petrified lucky date."

"A petrified lucky *what*?" Sophie blinked.

"Date. You know, they come from palm trees and are considered a delicacy? Of course, I'm not saying they are as good as Cheetos, but they do have their moments," Malik said as he emptied a packet into his hand and crammed the remaining Cheetos crumbs into his mouth. Finally, he continued to speak. "Anyway, long before four-leaf clovers and rabbit feet, petrified lucky dates were all the rage."

"Yes, but what do they do?" Harvey looked confused.

"Why, they bring people good luck, of course." Malik looked at him like he was stupid. "I kind of thought it was implied in the title."

"You think a petrified lucky date will help me get Melissa to give me my djinn ring back?" Sophie asked to make sure she was hearing right.

"Well, first you have to get one," Malik reminded her. "Last time I checked, Rufus was charging fifty bucks, which, if you ask me, is a little steep. Besides, how else are you going to make things right between Ben and Melissa if you don't have your magic *or* a lucky date?"

"I don't know, but I guess I'll just have to figure something out," Sophie said in a positive voice while trying to ignore just how disastrous the day was becoming. Thankfully, before she could think about it further, the whistle blew, and the team jogged out into the middle of the basketball court.

Once again, Sophie started searching for Jonathan.

But before she could find him, her hand flew up to her eyes and covered them. If he had looked surprised to see her pulling faces at him before, he must've been really shocked to see this. Unfortunately, thanks to her fingers, she couldn't see his expression.

She desperately tried to pull her hand away, but she couldn't budge it.

"Er, Sophie. Why do you have your hand over your eyes?" Harvey asked in a low voice. "Because not that I care what people think, but they are starting to look at you funny."

"I can't help it," Sophie started to say before remembering Melissa's last command. *In fact, I don't even want you to look at him again until you've fixed things with Ben and me.* Sophie slunk further down into the bleachers and let out a long groan, her eyes still covered. And here she was thinking that things couldn't possibly get any worse.

14

AYBE HE DIDN'T NOTICE?" KARA SAID IN A KIND voice as they all piled onto the bus once the game was finished.

"I had my hands across my eyes for the entire game. Even Mr. Morton the janitor noticed, and he's half blind," Sophie wailed as she rubbed her temples and reminded herself that it was lucky she was a positive thinker, since she was pretty sure that any other eleven-year-old who had been forced to sit through a basketball game looking like an idiot—*while her crush was playing*—would've died on the spot. Whereas Sophie knew that the best thing to do was to look for the positive part of it all. She still hadn't found it yet, but given time she was sure she would.

"Yes, but when this is all over, you can just explain to him that you had something in your eye," Harvey said. "But right now we need to concentrate on getting Ben and Melissa back together. Which, for the record, goes against everything I believe in, since evil like that should never be encouraged."

"I know. It's hardly ideal, but we have to make it work," Sophie said as she glanced around. "Actually, I was hoping Ben would be on the bus so I could talk to him."

"I don't see him." Harvey, who was half a head taller than Sophie, craned his neck. "Maybe he went out with the rest of the team to celebrate their win?" Then he caught Sophie's look of alarm. "Or he might've gone to the library to study for his quiz tomorrow."

"It's going to be okay," Kara said in a soft voice as the bus pulled to a halt. "You just need to go and see him first thing tomorrow and explain to him why it's not Melissa's fault he failed his Spanish quiz and got benched. Then once you've convinced him, Melissa will be so happy that she'll give your ring back."

"I hope so," Sophie said as she waved good-bye to her friends and made her way up the front path. There was no sign of Malik, but Sophie was actually pleased to have a little bit of Malik-free time. Especially since she still had to finish redoing her history assignment to hand in tomorrow morning. She had stupidly thought that she could just reprint it from her computer before remembering too late that it wasn't on her computer because she had created the first one using magic. And it turned out that her magic didn't have a hard-drive backup, so she was going to have to do this assignment the hard way.

Then she still had to talk to Ben, get her djinn ring back, apologize to Jonathan for being a freak, fix the studio leak, and practice her transcendental conjuring so that she could see the Djinn Council on Saturday. Even for such a positive thinker, this was a very big to-do list.

"No."

"I beg your pardon?" Sophie said the following day as she stood in front of Ben Griggs. She'd been so busy working on all the reasons why Ben shouldn't blame Melissa for his failing his Spanish quiz that she'd forgotten to give any thought to what his answer might be.

"I said no. You want me to tell Melissa I'm sorry I blamed her, but I'm not sorry at all. She was the one who put the bad mojo on me. It's totally her fault."

"Yes, but she wasn't the one who put down the wrong answers," Sophie reminded him as a hint of panic bled into her voice. "It was nothing to do with Melissa *or* the guitar pick. It was you." However, Ben was oblivious to her logic, and Sophie couldn't help but appreciate the irony that, like Melissa, he didn't seem to have a better nature.

Normally, at this point she would've used her magic to bribe him with something, but, of course, thanks to his girlfriend—make that ex-girlfriend—using magic wasn't an option.

"Look, Campbell, there's just no way I'm saying sorry to her. Now if you don't mind, I need to go and get ready."

"Oh." Sophie nodded. "Of course. You mean that

you've got to get ready to retake the Spanish quiz. Sure. I understand, but just remember, if you pass it, it's because of your own merit, not because of something that Melissa or a guitar pick did for you. Er, so did you study much?"

"What? Why should I study for a quiz that I had in the bag before Melissa came along and ruined it? I'm going to see Sam Henderson. We've got this most awesome joke planned … *and why are you covering your eyes with your hands?*" he asked. Sophie let out a groan since she could only take it to mean that Jonathan Tait had just walked past.

Sophie desperately tried to pull her hands away from her face, but they wouldn't budge until she heard Harvey shuffle up next to her. She finally tugged her fingers from her eyes, but there was no sign of either Jonathan or Ben. She tried not to cry.

"I'm taking it he wouldn't agree," Harvey said as he studied her body language. Not that he needed to be much of an expert to figure out that slumped shoulders and quivering lips meant failure.

"Don't feel so bad," Malik said, suddenly appearing next to them. "At least you got your history assignment handed in, and apart from all the weird stuff you wrote about Gallipoli, it was pretty good."

"Malik, I don't care about the history assignment," Sophie said while trying to ignore the fact that once again Jonathan must think that she hated him. "There is no way

Ben is going to pass that quiz. This is such a disaster. I wish I could sneak into his class and do it for him. Well, actually," she corrected herself, thinking of her less-than-stellar Spanish abilities, "if only Harvey could go in and do it for him, then he would be sure to pass."

"*Gracias.*" Harvey gave her a reluctant grin before frowning again. "Unfortunately, since I'm not invisible, I don't think that plan will work. Maybe we should concentrate on convincing Melissa again?"

"Hang on a minute." Malik suddenly looked up. "I'm invisible—well, not to you guys—but to everyone else."

"I certainly hope so." Sophie quickly glanced around to check that no one was looking at them as if they were talking to a Zac Efron look-alike ghost. However, no one seemed unduly interested in them and so she turned her attention back to Malik. "But what are you talking about? Is this another one of your ideas that involves magic?"

"No. I was thinking that I could go and help Ben with the Spanish quiz. It would be the helpful thing to do." Malik clapped his hands together, clearly impressed with his idea.

"Are you saying that you want to help him cheat?" Sophie leaned forward to check she was hearing right.

"Of course not. Cheating goes against all of my ethics as an ex-djinn who is now recently deceased and come back to life as a ghost."

"Last week you stole Meg's candy because you were

feeling hungry. You don't have any ethics," Sophie patiently reminded him. "But that's not what I meant. I just don't understand how you could help Ben pass if he doesn't even know that you're there?"

"Oh. That's actually very easy. You see, Eric the Giant taught me this trick where I can help guide a mortal's hand. I haven't used it before because—*regardless of what you think*—I'm very ethical. Okay, and yes, I admit that I have to concentrate really hard and it gives me a headache. Anyway, it works like this." As he spoke, he reached out and gently nudged Harvey's hand toward his backpack, and the next thing they knew, Harvey was pulling out a packet of Cheetos and handing it over to Malik.

"What the—" Harvey protested as his hand suddenly dropped back down into his lap and Malik happily opened up the Cheetos. Harvey stared at him in wide-eyed confusion. "How did you do that?"

"I'm afraid that is a confidential djinn secret, which I couldn't possibly tell you." Malik shrugged as he started to cram the cheesy snacks into his mouth. "So what do you think? Is it or is it not a stroke of genius?"

"I don't know." Sophie felt the sweat start to bead on her upper lip. It wasn't that she didn't trust Malik, it was just—*okay, it was* totally *that she didn't trust him*. However, she quickly realized that she was running out of options. "So do you even speak Spanish?"

"Un poco," Malik said.

"Fine." Sophie let out a sigh and hoped that whatever he said actually meant, "Yup, I'm totally fluent." "Try to help him pass his quiz. Please, Malik, I really need this to work."

"I'll do my best," he assured her, his face looking oddly serious. Sophie crossed her fingers. What she wouldn't give for her Neanderthal Joe guitar pick right now—she had the feeling she was going to need all the luck she could get.

Sophie fiddled with her pen as she looked up at the clock on the wall. Harvey had once tried to explain to her and Kara that, according to Einstein, time was relative, and it went as quickly or as slowly as you wanted it to go. But if that was the case, then could someone please explain why the bell still hadn't rung, when Sophie could swear that she'd been sitting in Mrs. Dobson's English class for at least three hundred years. There was nothing relative about it. It was just torture, pure and simple.

Next to her Kara was looking equally fidgety as she drew a series of small circles that twirled and intertwined with one another, while on the other side of her Harvey was listing his top ten favorite horror movies and trying not to grind his teeth. *And still the bell didn't ring.*

Sophie took a deep breath and started to tap her pen against her cheek as she once again wondered how Malik was getting on. Even the idea of sending him out to help Ben made Sophie nervous, since Malik seemed to find trouble like a moth found a flame. Unfortunately, she didn't have a lot of other options left.

Then there was the whole Jonathan thing, which had not gotten any better during the rest of the day. She longed to talk to him, but thanks to Melissa's command, she couldn't get near him without shutting her eyes and covering them with her hand. Kara and Harvey had seen him at lunchtime and explained that she was suffering from some weird eye allergy, but Sophie could tell by their unsmiling faces that they'd made the situation only worse.

Finally, the bell rang, and school was over for the day. Sophie immediately clapped her hands to summon Malik, before once again remembering that, until she got her ring back, her magic wouldn't work unless Melissa told her to do something.

She jumped to her feet and quickly thrust her books into her backpack before hurrying out into the crowded hallway. Kara and Harvey weren't far behind her. They all urgently craned their necks until Harvey finally pointed over to where Malik was hovering next to an unsuspecting Louise Gibson, who was about to take a bite of a Snickers bar.

They raced over, and Sophie managed to get her body in between Malik's outstretched hand and Louise's candy bar. The seventh grader shot Sophie a "you are such a freak" look before walking off, but Sophie hardly noticed. She eagerly turned to Malik, who was pouting about not getting the Snickers.

"So? How did it go? Did he pass? Can I get my ring back yet?"

"Sorry, I'm afraid it didn't go well." Malik shook his head. "In fact, it would be fair to say that Ben Griggs is the most spectacularly stupid mortal I have ever come across. I mean, I wrote the answers down for him, and what did he do? He crossed them out and wrote new ones in."

"Yes, but are you sure he failed? I mean, remember that what you think are the right answers might not necessarily be the 'real' right answers," Sophie reminded him, as visions of Moroccan almonds flittered into her mind.

"I think we can all agree that the translation for 'Where is the bus stop?' isn't 'Dude, showy me da bus place,'" Malik said in a dry voice. "Unless, of course, you're Ben."

"Oh." Sophie winced. "So he definitely failed?"

"In a stunning fashion," Malik reluctantly informed her. "I'm sorry. I really did try."

"I know, and I appreciate it. Besides, maybe Melissa doesn't know yet, and she will just change her mind about giving me back my ring?" Sophie asked in a hopeful voice, but next to her Kara shook her long dark hair.

"Judging by the look on her face, I'm going to guess that she knows."

"And doesn't look happy about it," Harvey added with a shudder as Melissa marched toward them, leaving a trail of fury behind her. Yup, she'd definitely heard.

"Melissa, hey. I was just coming to find you."

"Really? Are you sure you're not just trying to figure out another way to ruin my life?" the other girl retorted in a frosty voice. "Because I've just seen Ben, and now it's official. He dumped me. That's right, I've been dumped. And tomorrow there's a big squad practice at school, and the basketball team is going to be there as well. Do you have any idea how humiliating that's going to be? I mean, Ben will be there, and everyone will know. Oh, and did I mention that it's all your fault?"

Sophie wondered whether she should've just gone with the petrified lucky date after all. She shot Melissa a pleading look. "Okay, I know this sounds crazy, but if you would just give me my ring back, then I absolutely, totally promise that I will be able to fix this. In fact, I'll be able to get Ben as many lucky charms as he wants, and I'll make sure he knows that all his good luck has come from you."

"Um, no." Melissa shook her shiny blonde hair and narrowed her eyes until they were just two thin slits. "I think you've done quite enough damage for one day. Now get out of my way, loser."

"What? No—" Sophie started to protest, since she couldn't afford to take no for an answer. Unfortunately, her feet seemed to have other ideas, and the second Melissa told her to get out of the way, Sophie found herself turning and heading in the other direction, where her friends were waiting for her.

None of them bothered to say a word as they numbly trudged to the bus. Even the other kids around them didn't seem to speak. It was like they all knew that Sophie was going through some kind of personal apocalypse. She could vaguely see her friends exchanging concerned looks, but it wasn't until the bus came to a halt and they all clambered off that Kara finally spoke.

"Would you like us to come in with you? We could do some research on the Internet. You've still got until tomorrow at ten and—"

"There's no point." Sophie gave a resigned shake of her head as Melissa's stubborn eyes seemed to dance in front of her face as a constant reminder that Sophie had screwed up.

"Sophie, I'm really sorry." Malik's normally unperturbed face was set into frown mode.

"Seriously, I'm fine—well, I'm not fine, but it's not the end of the world. I-I guess I'll just have to find another way to find out what happened to my dad," Sophie said in an overly bright voice, which was at odds with how frozen she really felt. Whoever said that misery loved company was lying. Misery was just as happy to sit in a room on its own so that it could brood and sulk and listen to Neanderthal Joe songs over and over again on shuffle. "Do you guys mind?"

"Of course not." Harvey nodded.

"But make sure you call or IM us if you need anything," Kara added before the two of them headed to their own houses. Once they had left, Malik looked at her in concern.

"Are you really just going home? I mean, I don't always get this positive-thinking stuff of yours, but I thought you would be trying to figure this out until the end."

"Maybe I've realized that a perky affirmation isn't going to fix this," Sophie said in a flat voice as she shrugged. "Anyway, you don't need to stay. Why don't you go and hang out with Eric or something?"

For a moment Malik looked like he was going to say something, but then he merely shrugged his shoulders and disappeared from sight. Once he was gone, Sophie pushed the door open. There was no one around, so she slipped quietly up to her room.

As soon as she shut the door, she put her iPod on and started to listen to the playlist Jonathan had made for her. As she listened, she looked around her room. Everything about it looked so familiar, from the yellow-and-white walls, which were covered in Neanderthal Joe posters, to her computer table, which was filled with Malik's *High School Musical* memorabilia.

Except it wasn't the same anymore. Nothing was. She gritted her teeth and tried not to think of how badly she had screwed up. If she hadn't gotten herself bound, then she would be getting ready to see the Djinn Council tomorrow. She would be dazzling them with her powers, and then she would find out about her dad. Sophie felt a lump form in her throat as she sat down on the edge of her bed and tried not to think of what she was about to lose. But it was impossible. Her best shot at seeing her dad again was ruined, and there wasn't a thing she could do about it.

It's just it was all so unfair. Not just about her dad and her magic, but about Jonathan, too. Thanks to Melissa and her stupid commands, everything was ruined. The moment she and Jonathan had shared when Eddie Henry gave her the guitar pick. The playlists he kept making for her. Everything. All ruined.

She had failed.

15

SOPHIE WOKE UP ON SATURDAY MORNING TO A loud pounding noise. She clutched at her pillow and was just about to throw it at Malik and tell him to leave her alone when she heard her sister's voice at the door. She sat up with a start and did a quick check of her room to make sure there was nothing strange or djinn-ish lying around before she reluctantly called out for her to come in.

"Mom said that you need to come downstairs. It's time to throw out all of Dad's things." Meg folded her arms and looked sulky. Sophie let out a groan as she remembered yet another thing that she had failed to fix. And judging by her sister's face, Meg knew it as well.

"I'm so sorry," Sophie said as she scrambled out of bed and tried to squeeze her sister's hand, but Meg swiped it away and still looked upset. Not that Sophie could really blame her. In fact, Sophie had spent the whole night thinking about the mosh pit that her life had become. No wonder she felt so tired.

"No, you're not. You're just a big liar. You said you would fix it. I *wish* that you would fix it," Meg said in a fierce voice.

"I wish I could as well," Sophie said truthfully. She really, really wished it. Unfortunately, now her wishes didn't do any good. She could hear her mom making her way up the stairs, and so she reluctantly grabbed the first T-shirt and jeans she could see and got dressed. "Unfortunately, there's no magical solution to this, Meggy."

"I wouldn't say that." Her mom appeared in the doorway. However, instead of being dressed for a day of moving boxes, she was wearing a cute red dress with some black leggings under it. She had even brushed her hair. Sophie and Meg both stared at her. However, as usual, Meg was quicker to recover.

"What's going on?" she demanded, her shrewd eyes still studying their mom's neat appearance.

"I've just gotten off the phone with Max Rivers, and it looks like there's been a change of plan," their mom said with a grin as she walked over to Meg and gave her a big hug. "Not only has he given me a very large pottery order, but he doesn't think it's a good idea to work out of the basement because there's no natural light. Which is why he's offered me the use of the small workshop at the back of his antique store. Just until I can get the studio fixed, of course."

Sophie studied her mom's face just to check that she

was really hearing right. "So if you don't need to use the basement, does that mean—"

"That we don't need to sort out any more of the things down there. Including your father's boxes," their mom said with a smile.

"Really?" Sophie's voice was just above a whisper, since in a week of disaster, this small victory felt staggeringly good. It took all of her concentration not to cry out in relief.

"Really," her mom agreed. "Though I can't promise that we will keep them forever, but I can promise that we won't do anything with them until we're *all* ready."

"Thank you," Sophie said.

"Don't thank me. It was Max's kind offer that made it possible. I'm actually going to look at the workshop now, if you'd like to come with me."

"No, thanks." Meg immediately shook her blonde curls. "Because that sounds really boring. Besides, if we're not moving boxes, I can go over to Jessica's house. Her mom's going to make a chocolate shark cake today."

"Fine. Just mind your manners, and don't try to make Jessica play shark the entire time," their mom lectured.

"But she *likes* it," Meg assured her before racing out of the room and thundering down the stairs and out the back door.

"Well, that was easy. So what about you? Would you like to come with me?" her mom asked as she went over to the window to watch Meg scramble over the back fence and into the Daltons' yard.

"Actually, I'm not sure." Sophie's mood immediately plummeted as she remembered that today was when she was meant to be going to see the Djinn Council. Except, thanks to her losing her magic, she couldn't go. However, the idea of going to see her mom's ex-boss Mr. Rivers didn't exactly fill her with excitement. She'd have just as much fun sitting in her room sulking.

Her mom frowned as she cleared some clean laundry off Sophie's computer chair and sat down. "Is everything okay? You don't seem quite yourself this morning, and you were quiet last night at dinner, too. And while I understand how upset you were about throwing away your father's old things, I thought you would be a lot happier now."

Sophie felt her bottom lip start to tremble, and she took a deep breath to pull herself together. "I'm fine. I mean, I am happy. It's just I've just got a lot on my mind."

For a moment her mom paused and started to study Sophie's face thoughtfully. "Is this about the conversation we had the other day? When you were asking me if anyone had ever hated me?"

Sophie blinked for a moment in confusion before she realized her mom was talking about back when Melissa Tait had been just annoying, rather than been able to control Sophie's every move, and in turn ruin her life.

"Unfortunately, she still hates me." Sophie sighed,

since really that was at the heart of everything.

"Well, have you tried to talk to her?"

"It's not that simple." Sophie studied her fingers and tried to remember what her djinn ring even looked like. "She isn't exactly the kind of girl who likes to talk. Besides, it's too late."

"Sophie." Her mom looked at her in surprise. "That's not like you. What happened to your positive thinking? You're always the one who reminds me that we can change the world with our thoughts. And look what happened with the studio. You told me that a few days could make all the difference, and you were right. It's part of your magic."

Sophie felt her lip start to tremble again. "Trust me, Mom. I don't have *any* magic. I wish I did. Maybe then things would be different."

"You know your father always said that real magic happened here," her mom said as she touched her heart, and Sophie looked up sharply.

"D-dad talked to you about magic?"

"Well, not about real magic, obviously," her mom conceded, sounding quite surprised. "But yes, he did mention it from time to time. He said that people think magic is a physical thing that comes from the mind, but he thought it was heartfelt. Like how you got Meg and Jessica talking again. Your father would've said that was true magic." Then for a moment her voice wavered. "He also used to say that you and your sister were the two greatest pieces of magic he had ever done. Of course, I tried to tell him that I did all the hard work, but, well..." her mom trailed off, and for a moment they were both silent.

Sophie tried to make sense of what her mom had just told her. Not all magic was djinn magic. Some magic came from the heart.

Well, Sophie might not have her djinn ring anymore, but she still had a heart. For a moment she mulled over the possibility. *Could she really fix this without djinn magic?* Suddenly Sophie glanced at the time and jumped to her feet. She had no idea if she really could do it, but as a positive person she knew that she had to give it one final try.

Melissa had said she would be at cheerleading practice in the gym, and while Sophie had no idea what time it was going until, she figured that was the best place to start. Of course, if Melissa wasn't there, Sophie would be in trouble since she was due at the Djinn Council in an hour. But she would deal with that later.

"Actually, would you mind driving me to school on your way to Mr. Rivers's shop?" Sophie said as she grabbed a hoodie. "There's a big practice with the cheerleaders and basketball players going on."

"Cheerleading *and* basketball?" Her mom raised a surprised eyebrow, but Sophie just shrugged. "Are you sure you don't want to tell me what's really going on?"

"It's really long and complicated, but I sort of need to get there quickly. There's some magic that I need to do."

"I have no idea what I just managed to get across to you, but I'm pleased it worked." Her mom quickly got to her feet.

"It hasn't yet," Sophie said as they both rushed downstairs. From outside they could see that Meg was happily sitting in the Daltons' kitchen giving what appeared to be detailed directions on how to frost a shark cake. Sophie's mom exchanged a nod that seemed to contain a lot of information with Mrs. Dalton, and then she briskly walked to the car. Sophie gratefully followed her.

The Saturday morning traffic was light, and Sophie wasn't sure if it was because of the affirmation she was doing in her mind or because the traffic lights had a mind of their own, but they managed to hit only green lights the whole way over. In no time her mom was pulling the old Toyota up in front of Robert Robertson Middle School.

"Okay, so I'll go and see Max now, and I'll be back in an hour to collect you. Will that be enough time?"

"I hope so. And thanks, Mom," Sophie said before she gave her mom a fierce hug. "Wish me luck."

"You don't need luck, Sophie. You never have."

"I hope you're right," Sophie said as she jumped out of the car and raced toward the school. It didn't take her long to run down the empty hallways until she finally reached the gym. The sound of sneakers squeaking on the wooden floors and the dissonant echo of cheerleaders practicing their calls rang out as Sophie pushed the door open, which meant that the practice wasn't over yet. Well, that was good news, since this would definitely be harder to do if Melissa and Ben weren't there. *Not that she really had any idea what she was going to do—she just had to believe that it would work.*

She scanned the room, and out of habit her eyes immediately found Jonathan. Unfortunately, she couldn't see him, but she could tell he was there by the way her hand immediately flew up to her eyes. Sophie felt her good mood plummet. Part of her longed to go over to him and explain the whole lousy situation. Unfortunately, thanks to Melissa's earlier command, her feet stayed welded to the wooden floor. This was so annoying. Then she thought of what her mom had said.

Her dad believed there was other magic, more powerful than what a djinn could do. Suddenly, Sophie had an idea, and she fumbled around in her pocket with her spare hand until she found her iPod. She held it up in the air and waved at him. "Song number three," she called to him, not even sure if he was looking at her. And even if he was looking, would he know that she was talking about song number three on the playlist he'd given her? It was a Neanderthal Joe song called "Same Old Me," about a girl who goes away to college. At the start it looks like she's changed a lot, but underneath she's still the same skater girl in love with the boy next door.

"Oh, you've got to be kidding me," a voice suddenly said, and Sophie felt her fingers come away from her face just in time to see Melissa standing before her. Her blonde hair was pulled back in a ponytail, and she was looking as stylish and icy as ever in her cheerleading outfit. "I thought I told you to—"

"Enough." Sophie put her iPod back in her pocket and then held up her hand to stop Melissa from making any more commands. "I think you've done far too much talking, so for once I want you to shut up and listen. But first I need to find Ben."

"He's over there." Melissa sulkily pointed. "But he won't come over. He hasn't even looked at me once this morning. Not even when I did a backflip. And trust me, my flips are worthy of attention."

"Yeah, well, we'll see about that," Sophie retorted as she grabbed Melissa's hand and marched her over to where Ben was practicing his shooting.

"Hey, Campbell, have you heard the latest?" he demanded. "It's not bad enough that Coach is benching me for one game, now he's thinking of benching me for the entire season. Not just because of the Spanish quiz but because I can't get the ball in the hoop. Everything's gone south since she touched the guitar pick and ruined it." Then he shot the ball, and it hit the side of the hoop before dropping to the ground. "See? Jinxed."

"I keep telling you, you moron, if anyone jinxed you, Sophie did. Because—"

"Enough," Sophie suddenly commanded as she glared at both of them in annoyance. If it wasn't for these two, she wouldn't be avoiding Jonathan and she would be on her way to the Djinn Council to find out about her dad. Yet all they could do was stand there and blame each other. "You know what, Ben? Melissa is right. The only thing lucky about the guitar pick was that my favorite guitarist from my favorite band gave it to me. And you know the other reason I love it? Because Jonathan was there with me when it happened. So the only person that it meant anything to was me. To the rest of the world, it's just a piece of plastic that doesn't have any more magic in it than the stuffed ocelot that's the school mascot."

"See?" Melissa shot him a smug smile that Sophie ignored as she turned to Jonathan's twin sister.

"And you're not much better. So what if your boyfriend wants to touch my guitar pick? There's no reason to steal all of my jewelry and ruin my life just because you were jealous of something so ridiculous."

"But—" They both started to protest at once, but Sophie shook her head.

"No buts," Sophie admonished as she turned to Ben. "Now, you're going to pick up that basketball and shoot three hoops; if they all go in, then you're going to turn to Melissa and apologize for being such a muffin head. And you"—Sophie shifted her focus to Melissa—"are going to stop trying to meddle in things. He either likes you or he doesn't, but trust me, you can't make it happen just because you want it to happen. Are we clear?"

"No, because it's stupid. For a start, he's been missing

the hoop all morning, so what makes you think he's going to get it in now?" Melissa folded her arms and poked out her bottom lip in a sulk.

"Because there's no such thing as good luck or bad luck. It's all down to Ben, and since he likes you and he doesn't want to screw up anymore, he's going to make the shots. Isn't that right, Ben?"

"Well, I did like her before she put the jinx on me," he admitted before Sophie raised her eyebrows at him. "Fine. I'll shoot the stupid hoops."

At that moment Jonathan threw a basketball to him from across the court. Sophie didn't dare look at him because she didn't want to embarrass herself any further. Instead, she watched as Ben caught the ball and halfheartedly lined it up. He took the shot, and it went straight into the hoop without even hitting the backboard. Melissa made a small gasping noise.

"Huh." Ben seemed surprised as someone else threw him a second ball. This time he bounced it three times and then aimed and shot. Again, it went straight through the hoop. "Okay, did you see that? It went in twice, and I'm standing at the halfway line. I mean, seriously. It went in twice."

"Aren't you going to try to get it the third time?" Melissa asked in a surprisingly soft voice, but Ben shook his head as he shot her a goofy look.

"Actually, I don't think I need to. I think I get what Sophie was saying. I was dumb to think you were jinxing me; obviously, you're the one who was bringing me good luck."

Sophie stared at him. Had he not just heard her speech? There was no such thing as good luck—the only reason the ball had gone in was because he had wanted it to. However, before she could say anything, Melissa let out a distinctly goofy-sounding sigh.

"Really?" Melissa squeaked as she stepped toward him.

"Really," he said as he moved closer to her. They both seemed completely oblivious to the fact that they were standing in the middle of the Robert Robertson Memorial basketball courts about to kiss. Then Sophie wrinkled her nose. If they were about to kiss, did that mean she had—

"Oh, by the way, Sophie," Melissa's voice suddenly broke through her thoughts. "You can have this back. Costume jewelry is so last year." And without another word she tossed an apple-shaped, rhinestone-studded ring into the air and turned her attention back to Ben. Sophie gasped as she held out her hands to catch it. Unlike when she tried to catch a basketball, she managed to grab the ring without even fumbling.

As she slid it back on her finger she felt a surge of energy go racing through her. She looked at the time. It was one minute to ten, so without another word Sophie hurried from the gymnasium and clapped her hands for Malik to appear. She had done it.

16

OKAY, SO TELL ME WHAT THEY SAID. DID THE BIG ONE with the big spotty nose chew on her lip? Because that's a really bad sign, since whenever she chews her lip, some djinn gets beheaded. Oh, and did you remember to say 'thank you'? And please, please, please, tell me that you didn't make any jokes, because the Djinn Council has absolutely no sense of humor whatsoever."

"Malik." Sophie put a reassuring hand on his arm as they sat in the waiting room of the Djinn Council chambers. Well, it was where his arm was supposed to be, but since he was actually a ghost, it felt like she was patting thin air. "You don't need to worry."

"Of course I need to worry," he insisted. "Especially since they wouldn't even let me go into the chamber with you in case I tried to help you. It's like they don't trust me."

Sophie resisted the urge to grin as she reassured him. "I did everything you told me to do. I said thank you to all of them, and then I performed three different magical feats, including a very cool transcendental thing where I made one of the chairs do backflips all the way across the room. *While I was sitting in it.* And you know, if I do say so myself, I think it went pretty well."

"Yes, but that's just what they want you to think. It's the oldest trick in the djinn book," he said as he twiddled his thumbs and once again anxiously looked around the room. "Be nice and kind to the newbie, and then wham bam, you find yourself sent to Siberia with only a very lightweight polar fleece for protection. *And why are they taking so long to decide?*" Malik protested as he glanced at the large clock on the wall.

Unfortunately, it had three faces and twelve hands, and Sophie didn't have a clue what it said. As for her own watch, which Melissa had finally given back, it said that it was only one minute after ten, even though she was sure they had been there for at least an hour. Malik had tried to explain how time worked differently in the djinn dimension, but as far as Sophie was concerned, his explanation sounded a bit too much like something her math teacher might say, so she had zoned out.

"I don't know." She shook her head as she thought back to her interview. Her first shock had been to discover that the reason Malik had often described the Djinn Council as a bunch of old women was because they were, in fact, a bunch of old women. They also were just as scary as he had led her to believe. But funnily enough, after having to spend the last few days dealing with Melissa Tait and her arctic gazes, Sophie hadn't felt remotely scared. And as for the demonstrations they'd asked her to do? Well, even though it had been a while since she'd used any magic, she quickly discovered that it was just like riding a bike, but without the ugly helmet or the uncomfortable seat.

"Well, I do," Malik continued, still looking agitated. "It's because they'd decided to say no, and you know what? That's not good enough. In fact, I think I'm going to go in there and give them a piece of my mind right now. So what if I'm not the most fabulous djinn who was ever created from smokeless fire, I'm still Malik the Great, and that has to stand for something. Oh, and you know, they'd better not hold the whole getting-bound thing against you, because I'll tell you what, the way you managed to negotiate your way out of that was pure genius. In fact, you could probably even manage to get yourself unbound from Sheterum himself, and furthermore—"

"Who's Sheterum?" Sophie blinked, trying to keep up with Malik's rambling, as her grip tightened on the small silver box that her dad had given her and which was now perched in her lap.

"What?" Malik paused for a moment and gave a dismissive wave of his hand. "Oh, he's this techno-sahir who uses the Internet to track down and bind djinns. Hateful fellow. Almost up there with Solomon. Anyway, where was I? Oh, yes, if they think for one minute that they can—"

"Er, Malik." Sophie tried to nudge him as one of the

old women from the Djinn Council suddenly floated out, holding a piece of paper. However, since he was noncorporeal, her nudge didn't work, and he kept on talking.

"No, I mean it, Sophie. Even though you didn't know I was on the basketball court with you because I was invisible, I heard the whole speech you gave to Melissa and Ben, and it was very moving. Especially the part where you told them what the guitar pick meant to you. The way you were emoting. You know, they could make that into a movie—oh, and Zac Efron could play me. Plus—"

The old woman djinn was now glaring at Malik through a pair of thick bifocals as she made a clicking noise with her false teeth.

"Seriously, Malik, enough." Sophie tried to catch his attention again, this time by waving her hand in front of his face. "I think the waiting is over."

"What?" He blinked for a moment before he glanced over to where the old woman was still hovering. His lip curled in distaste. "Oh, it's you, Farizad. I should've known."

"Malik." The old woman gave a curt nod of her head. "I can see that death hasn't stopped you from mouthing off at all. Anyway, the council has made a decision, so if Sophie, daughter of Tariq, would like to come with me, she can hear it."

"Yeah, well, don't try and stop me from coming in this time, because I won't stand for it. As her djinn guide I have a right to be there, and you'd better not try to stop me, Farizad, because we're not in Persia anymore." Malik poked his bottom lip out much the way he did when Sophie wouldn't conjure him up any more Cheetos.

"No one's trying to stop you, Malik, you big baboon. Now come on, the early bird bingo starts soon, and you know how I hate to miss that," the old woman djinn pronounced as she floated back into the council chambers, where Sophie had done her demonstration. The walls were covered with dark wooden carvings. Richly colored tapestry rugs were hanging everywhere, and a heavy smell of incense filled the air.

The cool tiled floor was dotted with decorative earthen pots filled with delicate palms, and in the center of the room was a selection of large cushions, which hadn't been there before. The old woman gestured for Sophie to take a seat while she joined the rest of the council members, who, instead of sitting on cushions, were all in large leather recliners that Sophie was pretty sure had come from Pottery Barn.

"Sophie, daughter of Tariq, we have witnessed your skills and considered your request. And we have decided to help you."

"You have?" Sophie widened her eyes as her heart started to pound in nervous excitement, while next to her Malik's jaw went slack in surprise. "D-does that mean you know where my dad is?"

"Unfortunately, we don't know where he is, but there are two things that we can tell you. First, he is still alive;

and second, he has been bound by a sahir named Shet-erum."

"Sheterum?" Sophie repeated in shock. That was the guy Malik had just been talking about. "The techno-sahir?"

"I see you've heard of him." Another of the Djinn Council members nodded. This old woman was as fat as a house, with wispy gray hair pulled back from her face and a few unpleasant-looking stray hairs on her chin.

"S-so how do I unbind him?" Sophie demanded. She felt the blood pound in her temples, but the members of the Djinn Council just looked at her blankly.

"That is not our concern. Malik will tell you what we think of djinns who get themselves bound," Farizad said in a sharp voice as she glanced up at another one of the strange-looking clocks. "And now, it is time for you to leave. More importantly, it's time for bingo."

"What? No." Sophie shook her head as she watched the twelve old women start to hover up from their recliners. "You can't go. I need more help. And what about opening this box? It could have something important in it."

"Oh, yes." Farizad paused for a moment and lifted a gnarled, arthritic-looking finger in the air. Sophie felt the box being tugged out of her hands, and she watched as it flew across to where Farizad was hovering. The old woman then snapped her fingers, and the silver lid effort-lessly flipped back. Farizad eagerly peered inside it and pulled out a carefully folded parchment of paper. Then she frowned as she tried to read it. Finally, she looked up. "Malik, you spent a lot of your dissolute years around mortals. What does this say, and is it in Tariq's hand?"

"A letter from my father?" Sophie immediately jumped to her feet, but one of the other old women raised a finger, and instead of crossing the cool tiled floors, Sophie felt herself being pushed back down into the cushions by an invisible force. She tried to wriggle free, but it was no good, and she was forced to watch helplessly as Malik floated over to where Farizad was holding on to the piece of paper.

"Well?" the old lady demanded. "What does it say?"

Malik paused for a moment and scanned it before he turned and shot Sophie an apologetic look. "I'm sorry, Sophie. It's not a letter. It's a recipe."

"A recipe?" Farizad sounded almost as disappointed as Sophie felt. "Are you sure?"

"Of course I'm sure." Malik bristled. "It's for spaghetti Bolognese. In case you didn't know, Tariq was quite the cook. Huh, well, will you look at that, his secret ingredient is nutmeg. Interesting."

"Interesting?" Farizad spat in disgust. "You're just as bad as Tariq himself. He was once a brilliant djinn, but instead of working with the council to unleash his true potential, he turned his back on us and married a mere mortal. And look at him now: bound by one of the worst sahirs in our recent history and his only legacy is a recipe."

"How dare you speak like that about my mom and my

dad?" Sophie felt a flash of rage go racing through her as once again she tried to stand up, but whatever was restraining her only tightened its grip.

"Sophie, daughter of Tariq, we will speak as we please, and you will show us respect," the bearded old lady retorted. Then, without another word, the old women all floated out of the room, no doubt in the direction of the bingo hall. As soon as they were gone, whatever had been restraining Sophie suddenly disappeared, and she jumped to her feet.

"Malik, we need to go after them. How am I supposed to find my father without their help?" she demanded.

Malik shook his head. "I'm sorry, Sophie, but once the council members have made their decision, there's no changing their minds. And at least you know he's alive. Plus, he left you this lovely recipe, so I suggest we go home and try to make it."

Sophie stared at Malik in disbelief as he waved the piece of paper in front of her face. Was he kidding her? "I don't want to make spaghetti, I want to find my dad. I thought you were my friend. I can't believe you're not going to help me. Hey—" she started to say as she stared at the recipe in confusion. "This isn't—"

"This isn't the right place to talk about spaghetti?" Malik quickly cut her off. "I completely agree," he said in an extra loud voice, as if someone was listening. "Besides, looking at all those old djinns has given me a headache, which is why we should get going. Plus, Zac Efron is on

Ellen today, and if you think I'm going to miss that, then you've got another think coming." Then he clicked his fingers, and the next thing Sophie knew, they were both outside the Robert Robertson Middle School gymnasium again.

Sophie blinked and then looked at her watch. It was two minutes past ten, which meant that somehow she had been away for only a couple of minutes. She had no idea how it was possible, but it was obviously part of the whole "Djinn Council being on a different dimension" thing. Not that it was her biggest worry right now. She looked at the piece of paper in her hand and then looked up at Malik, unable to hide her confusion.

"What's going on? Why did you tell the council that this was a spaghetti recipe when it's really all about Solomon's Elixir? And, hey—" She suddenly frowned. "Is that the elixir that you said doesn't exist?"

"It doesn't, *well, it didn't*," Malik replied, his voice tinged with excitement. "But according to this, it looks like your father might've managed to find a way to make it. Don't you see, not only was your dad a great cook, but he might've been on the verge of discovering the secret that every djinn for two thousand years has been searching for?"

"But I still don't understand." Sophie frowned. "Why didn't you tell the Djinn Council about it? I mean, wouldn't they want to know about it?"

"Of course they would, but let me tell you something

about the Djinn Council. They may look like a bunch of old ladies who could use a dip in a tub of Nair and a visit to the mall, but underneath it all they are powerful djinns. And the one thing that powerful djinns like more than anything else in the world is more power."

"And you think that if this really does turn out to be the elixir, it would be powerful?"

"More powerful than any of the other trinkets they currently have in their coffers," Malik confirmed. "And more to the point, if you gave it to them, there is absolutely no guarantee that they would let you use it to help your father."

"But we don't even know where he is. Maybe we could've done a trade with them for information or something?"

"Haven't I told you that you should never do deals with other djinns?" Malik reminded her as he made a tut-tutting noise from between his teeth. Then he grinned. "Besides, you can stop looking so gloomy, because I promised you that *finding* your dad was always going to be the easy part, it was the getting him unbound that would've been tough. But now—"

"Now we stand a chance." Sophie suddenly returned his grin: she finally understood why he was looking so happy. Then she turned and started to head down the hallway to wait for her mom out in the parking lot. It sucked that Sophie couldn't tell her that she was one step closer to finding her dad, but hopefully the time would come when she wouldn't have to tell her anything. Instead, she could actually bring her dad back, and then they would be a proper family again. The thought made her smile.

17

WOW, I STILL CAN'T BELIEVE IT." KARA SHOOK HER head in astonishment on Monday morning. "I mean, I thought I lost half an hour of my life last week when I was trying to finish Colin's tail and the glue I was using wouldn't stick, but you *literally* lost time. I mean, you said you were gone for over an hour, but it was only two minutes later when you got back."

"Not to mention that you found out that your dad is still alive, and now you have a way to break his bind," Harvey added. "Though, you know, it's kind of a pity that you didn't have the recipe sooner. It would've saved you a lot of stress."

"I know," Sophie agreed. "But on the positive side, if I'd had the elixir to break the bind, then I might never have figured out that sometimes I can fix a problem without actually using magic."

"Could you just excuse me while I puke," Malik chimed in from where he was lying across the top of a bank of lockers, peering down on them all. "Because if that isn't the cheesiest thing I've ever heard, then I don't know what is. Next you're going to tell me that you spent the whole night doing your geography assignment by yourself just because it's the right thing to do." Then he let out a disgusted groan. "*You did, didn't you? Honestly, sometimes I think I should just wash my hands of you.*"

"You watch *High School Musical*, and you're calling *me* cheesy? Besides, after the Moroccan almond debacle and the catastrophe of losing my magic, I didn't want to push my luck," Sophie protested as she stifled a yawn and clutched her freshly printed assignment. Anyway, Malik could say what he liked; not relying on her magic so much was actually quite empowering. In fact, from now on she was going to think twice before she even considered using magic again, unless it was a total emergency.

"Well, I think it's great," Kara said. "And really, all that matters is that things turned out just the way Sophie wanted them to."

"Absolutely." Sophie grinned as she hugged her assignment close to her chest. Her friend was right. For the last four years all she had dreamed of was her dad coming home, and now it looked like all of her positive thinking and affirmations were finally paying off. In fact, everything was completely and utterly perfect—

"Earth to Sophie," Kara's voice suddenly cut through her thoughts. "Jonathan is looking this way. Are you going to talk to him?"

Apart from the whole Jonathan Tait thing.

Sophie groaned as she glanced over to see Jonathan standing next to his locker looking grim. It wasn't exactly that she had forgotten about what had happened last week—she had just kind of hoped that if she ignored it enough, it would go away. But judging by the lack of a smile on Jonathan's gorgeous face, she was guessing that it hadn't gone very far.

Well, that sucked.

Especially since, despite the fact that she had a very good explanation for why she had been covering her eyes every time she saw him, it wasn't exactly one that she could tell him. Sophie licked her lips and took a deep breath. She should probably go over and talk to him and say, well . . . actually, she had no idea what she should say, but hopefully she would figure something out. And if he didn't want to have anything to do with her on account of the fact that she was a freak who had avoided him just because his twin sister had told her to, that was the chance she would have to take.

She cautiously smiled at him. The minute she did so, Harvey, Kara, and Malik melted away (well, Kara and Harvey melted, Malik made a loud snorting noise and then declared that if this was how it was going to end, he would prefer to go watch *High School Musical*, and then he disappeared from sight).

Sophie checked her hair as she made her way across the hallway to where Jonathan was standing. It was as flat as ever, and she quickly made a wish to give it a bit more body. (*What?* If fixing your hair when you were about to talk to your crush, who probably hated you, wasn't necessary and appropriate use of djinn magic, then she didn't know what was.)

Too soon she was standing in front of him. He was wearing a plain black T-shirt, and his hands were thrust deep into the front pockets of his jeans. Sophie couldn't help but notice that he was also clenching and unclenching his jaw as he rocked back and forth on his feet. Suddenly, she wished that Harvey was still there to tell her what jaw clenching and rocking meant. Was it a nervous thing? An "I'm mad as anything at you" thing? Or something else entirely?

She also wished that she had come up with an explanation for why she had been acting like a total freak for the last few days. Because unfortunately, right now she had nothing.

"Hey, Sophie," he finally spoke as he stopped the jaw clenching.

"Hey," she gulped in reply before nervously licking her lips and avoiding eye contact. "Look, I'm not really sure how to explain what happened last week."

"Yeah." He nodded his head before he finally looked at her. "Okay, so here's the thing. If you like Ben, then just tell it to me straight up."

"What?" Sophie, who had been desperately trying to

figure out what to say next, paused for a moment to check that she had heard right. "You still think that I like Ben? Didn't you see him and your sister on Saturday morning?"

Jonathan shrugged, still looking a bit pained. "Just because he likes someone else doesn't mean it stops how you feel."

"I guess not, but I absolutely don't like Ben. How can you even think that?"

"It's not really that crazy. Every time I saw you, you were talking to him, and to make it worse, you kept covering your eyes as if you were cutting me dead. And"— he stopped for a moment and did more jaw clenching— "you took off the guitar pick. I guess when I saw that you weren't wearing it anymore, it just kind of hit me. This is going to sound dumb, but when we were at the concert and Eddie Henry gave it to you, it felt to me like we had a moment—"

"It did? Because that's exactly what I thought," Sophie exclaimed in an excited voice before realizing that people were starting to look at them. She lowered her voice. "I mean, about having a moment. I thought that, too."

"Really? So why did you take it off then?" he wanted to know, his dark eyes now steadily staring into hers.

"It's a long story." Sophie chewed at her lip as she tried to ignore just how tempting it was to put Melissa right in the middle of it. Unfortunately, her better half won out, and she just shrugged. "But the short version is that I lost it."

"It's not lost." Jonathan shook his head as he awkwardly pulled something out of his pocket and held it up. Sophie gasped as she realized he was holding up a delicate silver chain with the familiar-looking guitar pick hanging off it.

"You found it?" Sophie continued to stare at it as he carefully started to undo the tiny catch. "I don't believe it. I didn't think I'd ever see it again."

"I found it last week before school. It was in a trash can near my locker," Jonathan admitted. "I just wasn't sure if you wanted it back or not. In fact, I was pretty certain you didn't, but then on Saturday at basketball, when you got me to listen to the third song on the playlist? I guess I hoped you'd changed your mind."

"My mind never needed changing," Sophie assured him as she realized he had opened the clasp and was waiting to see if he could put it back around her neck. "It was just a series of freak-crazy things that happened, and I swear that if I have my way, they will never happen again."

"I'll second that. No more freak-crazy things." He grinned as he tentatively walked around behind her to put the chain on. Even better, because she was so short he easily slid it around her neck and carefully did the clasp. The minute the delicate silver chain touched her collarbone, Sophie started to smile. She spun around to face Jonathan again, and they headed down the hallway together. As they went, he nudged her with his elbow. She nudged him back and continued to smile.

Magic or no magic, things had ended up turning out just the way she had wanted them to. Now that's what she called positive thinking.

Turn the page for a peek at the next book...

Sophie's
MIXED-UP
Magic

Out of
Sight

BOOK 3

1

SOLOMON'S ELIXIR.

Sophie Campbell's fingers tightened around the tiny vial of amber liquid, which shimmered and sparkled like the sun rising over the Sahara Desert. Well, okay, so Sophie hadn't ever seen the sun rising over the Sahara Desert, but Malik, her ghostly djinn guide, had assured her that it was completely identical, minus all the locusts. Not that it really mattered what the liquid looked like; the important thing was that it was not only the most sought-after magic in the djinn kingdom, it was also the key to freeing her father from the binds of Sheterum, an evil sahir. The idea made Sophie feel giddy, because the sooner her dad was freed, the sooner they could be a proper family again.

Her smile faded slightly.

Unfortunately, there was one small chink in her very good plan. In order for the elixir to free her father, she needed to find out where he was being held, and that was proving to be a problem. A big problem. Thankfully, Sophie was a positive person and she was sure that the Universe wouldn't have helped her find all of the ingredients to make the elixir (including eel-tail oil extract, which, for the record, stank worse than gym socks) if it wasn't going to help her find out where her father was being held.

And so Sophie slipped the precious vial back into the pocket of her jeans as she made her way through the crowded backstage area of the Robert Robertson Middle School auditorium on Monday afternoon.

"Sorry, I'm late." She puffed as she came to a halt alongside her two best friends, who were standing next to a papier-mâché flying monkey called Colin. Sophie widened her eyes. "Wow, he looks amazing."

"I know, right," Kara agreed as she flipped a strand of long dark hair out of her face and carefully inspected one of the wings to make sure it was okay. Kara, who was the artist of the trio, had spent the last couple of weeks up to her elbows in glue and newspaper making props for the upcoming musical, *The Wizard of Oz*.

"Well, I just hope that they're using lots of ropes on him, because if he falls someone is going to get seriously splattered. I saw this movie once where that exact thing happened," Harvey, the movie buff of the three, said as he knit his brows together.

"Colin isn't going to be splattering anyone," Kara cut him off before he could talk about anything too gruesome. Then she turned back to Sophie and wrinkled her nose. "Anyway, where have you been? The dress rehearsal starts in five minutes. I was starting to think that you'd forgotten about it."

"Of course I didn't forget about it." Sophie looked horrified as she wiped the sweat away from her brow and silently concluded that if she had to keep running around school like this, she was going to have to get a lot fitter. "You know that I would never let you down like that."

"Well, that's good." Kara looked relieved as she fiddled with one of Colin's monkey ears. "I'm so nervous about Colin's big day."

"She's not exaggerating," Harvey confirmed as he held out his arm. "She's been pinching me for the last ten minutes to help her calm down. I'm sure I'm going to have a bruise tomorrow. So what happened? Did you get distracted by Jonathan?"

At the mention of Jonathan Tait's name, Sophie let out a happy sigh, since she thought the seventh grader, with his tanned skin and blond hair, was the most perfect guy in the whole entire world. Plus, he loved Neanderthal Joe almost as much as Sophie did and they had sortofkindofmaybe been hanging out together ever since she had started sixth grade last month. Then she realized her two friends were looking at at her expectantly, so she lost the dreamy expression and gave a quick shake of her head.

"No, it didn't have anything to do with Jonathan," she

assured them. "It's just that on my way here I noticed that the cafeteria was serving meatloaf."

"Meatloaf?" Kara squeaked, her normally relaxed face suddenly looking far from happy. "You nearly missed Colin's first proper rehearsal because of some meatloaf?"

"Well, in Sophie's defense, the cafeteria here does make very good meatloaf," Harvey offered. "Much better than what we got at Miller Road Primary, that's for sure. Apparently they've got a special secret. *What?*" he protested as he suddenly realized the two girls were staring at him. "It's true."

"We believe you," Sophie quickly assured him before she turned back to Kara, who was glancing nervously around the backstage area. "But what I mean is that I've been looking for Malik. He promised he would be here by now, so when I saw that the cafeteria was doing meatloaf I thought he might've snuck in there to steal some."

Her friends both nodded knowingly—stealing meatloaf from the cafeteria was exactly the sort of thing that Malik was likely to do. Unfortunately, ever since Sophie herself had become a djinn, she had been stuck with him as her djinn guide. Not that he did much guiding. Instead he spent most of his time watching YouTube clips, eating Cheetos, and getting Sophie into trouble. Usually all at the same time. Unfortunately, he was also the only hope she had of finding out where her father was.

"So, I gather that Malik wasn't there," Kara said, her voice full of understanding.

"No." Sophie let out a frustrated sigh. "I even checked behind the deep fryer where they were cooking the meatloaf, but there was no sign of him."

"Ah, so that's the secret to the meatloaf. Deep-frying. Nice." Harvey, who was a big fan of eating, nodded his head in approval before he realized they were staring at him again, and so he coughed. "*But so not the point.* So have you tried clapping him?"

"I've been clapping him all morning," Sophie said, since according to Malik, clapping was like ringing a doorbell and when she did it he would appear. However, if this was true, then all she could conclude was that Malik's doorbell was broken. Very, very broken. "What if something's happened to him? What if—"

Before she could finish, Patrick Dutton, an emo-looking seventh grader with aqua eyes and Justin Bieber hair, strode toward them. He had a clipboard in one hand and what looked like part of the yellow brick road in the other. Kara immediately started to blush.

"Hey, Kara. The rehearsal is just about to start, but you can watch it from the front. And don't worry, I'll take good care of Colin for you," Patrick said with a wink. But instead of replying, Kara began to fiddle with her hair as she mumbled something that sounded very much like *mwhooahwwh*. Then, as Patrick carefully moved Colin over to the left side of the stage, Kara dropped her head and hurried to the front of the auditorium as fast as her long legs would take her. Sophie and Harvey exchanged a surprised glance before they raced after her.

"Um, excuse me, what's going on?" Sophie demanded as she finally caught up with her friend and they all sat down in an empty row of seats.

"Nothing. Nothing's going on," Kara said in a rush,and shot Sophie a concerned look.

"So why were you acting so—" Sophie started to say before widening her eyes. "Kara, do you have a crush on Patrick?"

"What?" Kara blinked as she studied her fingers, refusing to look up at either of her friends. "No, of course not. W-why would you think I had a crush on him? That's crazy talk."

"Er, because you did *this* and *this* when he was talking to you," Sophie said as she nervously tugged at her hair to demonstrate Kara's behavior. "Not to mention the whole *mwhooahwwh* thing. Is that even a word?"

"Oh no." Kara let out a long groan as her cheeks turned the color of ketchup. "So do you think that he noticed?"

"Only if he had ears and eyes," Harvey assured her. Sophie hit him in the arm.

"Of course he didn't, and the only reason we noticed was because we know you so well," Sophie quickly backtracked as she realized that Kara *did* have a crush on Patrick. Why hadn't Kara told her? But she already knew the answer. She had been so caught up with finding her dad and the whole djinn thing that she hadn't realized Kara even knew Patrick, let alone liked him. She was a bad friend. "So why didn't you tell us you liked him?"

"Well, at first I didn't know I liked him. He's one of the stagehands, and he's been coming to the art room to check on Colin's progress," Kara explained as she nervously started to fiddle with her necklace. "And that's when I noticed the color of his eyes. I mean, did you see them? They were like the ocean on a summer's day with just a hint of lapis in there." She let out a dreamy sigh and her shoulders started to droop. "But of course it's hopeless. You saw me. I can't even string two words together when I'm around him. Why would he ever like me?"

"Um, because you are gorgeous, not to mention sweet, kind, and funny. Oh, and you're also very nice to papier-mâché flying monkeys," Sophie said. "And if you like him, then you should do something about it."

"W-ell, he did tell me that the whole drama club is going to see *The Wizard of Oz* at the movies on Saturday for inspiration. It's a sing-along. Anyway, he kind of asked me to go with them," Kara reluctantly admitted.

"He did not." Sophie widened her eyes as she gripped her friend's arm in excitement. "That's so majorly exciting!"

"Yeah, the thing is that I'm not so sure it would be a good idea." Kara shook her head. "What if I get all tongue-tied again and I'm stuck there on my own? I wish I could be more like you when you're around Jonathan. How do you manage to speak to him without feeling like you're going to melt into a puddle?"

"I don't know," Sophie said truthfully as she considered it. "I guess I'm always so excited to see him and then we're normally so busy talking about Neanderthal Joe that there's no time to be nervous. Perhaps you just need to make sure you talk about things you're interested in?"

"I guess." Kara still didn't look convinced, and Sophie felt another pang of guilt that she hadn't been more helpful to her friend. Then she had an idea.

"Hey, what if Harvey and I went with you? I mean I know that we're technically not part of the drama club, but it's a public movie theater so there's nothing to stop us from going too," Sophie said, and Kara immediately brightened.

"Really? You guys would do that?"

"Actually." Harvey coughed. "I can't. My mom's making me go along to some lame single-parent camp next weekend so we can bond with other single-parent families."

"Oh, Harvey, that's terrible." Sophie shot him a sympathetic look. His parents had recently split up and he was now caught right in the middle of all the warring.

"Tell me about it. I swear that my mom's only doing it to bug my dad because he wanted me to go to the lake with him. Honestly, parents are so complicated."

"So are they talking to each other yet?" Kara looked worried, and Harvey shook his long bangs.

"Not exactly, though they are talking *about* each other a lot. Mainly to me, so now I just put my earbuds in and nod from time to time. Something that I plan on doing the whole weekend while I'm away at Camp Touchy-Feely," he said as he blew his hair out of his eyes.

"Maybe it's a sign that I shouldn't go to the movie?" Kara said immediately, her pale green eyes full of worry. Sophie shook her head.

"You have to go. And even though Harvey can't make it, you've still got me. Oh, and we should get you a new outfit. You could ask your mom to take us to the mall. You know how excited she gets when you want to exchange your paint-splattered wardrobe for something new," Sophie said. Of course she would've been happy to conjure something up, but Kara's mom had a bad habit of noticing new clothes and wondering where they had come from.

"What? Oh please, not more crushes. I mean, first we had all the business with Sophie and Jonathan Tait, and now Kara likes someone? Honestly, I don't know where you kids ever get the time to just do your homework," a voice suddenly said. They all looked up to where Malik— Sophie's djinn guide—was now floating in front of them, a frown on his face.

Today he was wearing a bright yellow Hawaiian shirt and some skinny jeans, and his Zac Efron hair was slicked back off his head. He also had a bulky man bag slung over his shoulder, which he refused to stop using despite

Sophie's assuring him that it was the ugliest thing in the entire world. Thankfully, due to the fact that he was a ghost, Sophie and her friends were the only ones who could see him.

It was a small comfort.